JACKPOT

DON'T MISS ANY ANTICS OF THE MAN WITH THE PLAN, GORDON KORMAN:

SWINDLE

ZOOBREAK

FRAMED

SHOWOFF

HIDEOUT

JACKPOT

GORDON KORMAN

Scholastic Press • New York

Library of Congress Cataloging-in-Publication Data

Korman, Gordon.
Jackpot / Gordon Korman. — 1st ed.
p. cm. — (Swindle ; bk. 6)
Summary: Griffin Bing and his friends are trying to locate
Mr. Fielder's missing thirty million dollar lottery ticket, and thwart
the local bully, Darren Vader, who wants to find it for himself — and
Mr. Bing's latest invention may help.
ISBN 978-0-545-56146-4 (jacketed hardcover) — ISBN 978-0-545-56147-1
1. Lottery tickets — Juvenile fiction. 2. Inventions — Juvenile fiction.
3. Bullying — Juvenile fiction. 4. Friendship — Juvenile fiction.
[1. Lottery tickets — Fiction. 2. Inventions — Fiction. 3. Bullies —
Fiction. 4. Friendship — Fiction.] I. Title.
PZ7.K8369Jac 2014
813.54 — dc23
2013007882

10 9 8 7 6 5 4 3 2 1   14 15 16 17 18

Printed in the U.S.A. 23
First edition, January 2014

The text type was set in ITC Century.
Book design by Elizabeth B. Parisi and Whitney Lyle

For Henry and Reggie Korman

*S*tockholm, Sweden.

    "... *and this year's Nobel Prize in Physics is awarded to Professor Albert Einstein.*"

There was thunderous applause in the auditorium as Einstein came up to the podium to accept his gold medal.

Amazing, *thought Griffin Bing.* He didn't comb his hair, even for this.

The legendary genius took his seat on the platform beside Griffin as the ovation quieted.

"*Congratulations, Doc*," *Griffin whispered.*

"*And to you, young man*," *Einstein responded.*

"*Our next award*," *the master of ceremonies went on, "is a new prize for us. Our first-ever Nobel Prize in Planning goes to a teenage gentleman from Cedarville, United States — Griffin Bing.*"

Griffin rose, brushing off the satin lapels of his rented tuxedo. The place erupted with cheers, especially the front row, where his friends were sitting — Ben,

Pitch, Logan, Melissa, Savannah, and Luthor. They were all just as dressed up as he was, except for Luthor. They didn't make tuxedos for Dobermans, but clipped to his studded collar was a little black bow tie.

He felt a rush of gratitude toward them. They were the reason he was The Man With The Plan. No plan was worth anything without the right team to carry it out.

The auditorium resounded with celebration. It was a standing ovation! Fireworks went off — indoors! — with an earsplitting report.

Crack! Boom! Rat-tat-tat!

Crack! Boom! Rat-tat-tat!

Griffin came awake with a start, the Nobel auditorium popping like a soap bubble, along with his dream. His clock read 12:18. It was the middle of the night.

Crack! Boom! Rat-tat-tat!

He sat bolt upright in bed. The sound wasn't coming from any dream.

He rushed to the window and threw the blinds open just as another barrage of pebbles ricocheted off the glass. Someone was in the yard! He lifted the window, peered out, and hissed, "Who's there?"

"Hey, Bing — nice bedhead!"

Griffin squinted into the gloom. There behind a honeysuckle hedge stood a tall, burly eighth grader with pig eyes and a nasty sneer on his face. It was bad enough to be awoken from a super-great dream. But to be disturbed by the likes of Darren Vader was beyond annoying.

"Beat it, Vader!"

"Not till I show you this great thing I found." For the first time, Darren stepped into the open.

The wheeze that came from Griffin threatened to suck the neighborhood dry of all oxygen. Instantly, he recognized the contraption the boy was wearing. It resembled the white rectangular backpack that astronauts carry on their space suits, only this one was worn in the front. It was the SweetPick, Griffin's father's latest invention.

Mr. Bing had developed several agricultural devices designed for orchard harvesting. But the SweetPick was different. It was made for the sugar industry, to cut and bundle stalks of cane. Mr. Bing thought it might be his big break as an inventor, his first step out of the small orchard field into the wider food-production world.

"Vader, what are you doing with my dad's invention?"

No sooner had the words passed his lips than he knew: Darren's mother was Mr. Bing's lawyer. When the patent office had refused to approve the SweetPick, Mrs. Vader had taken the prototype to be professionally photographed for the follow-up application. Mr. Bing had brought it to her that very morning.

"What?" Darren was the picture of innocence. "This little thing? It's just some hunk of junk I found in the garage. Oh, wait, I forgot the most important part." He pulled a piece of paper from his pocket, unfolded it, and held it up against the device. He switched on a flashlight to make sure that Griffin could read it:

NOSEPICK

Griffin saw red. "You take that thing home to your mom, or I'm calling the cops!"

"Well, that would be really scary," Darren sneered, "except that it's not patented yet. So if I get arrested, everybody'll see the secret design. Dear old Dad won't be too happy about that, will he?"

Griffin was getting angrier by the second. "Put it back! It's one of a kind! If you break it —"

"Gee," Darren teased, "I wonder what this switch is for." He turned back to the honeysuckle and fingered the control that dangled from the pack.

"Don't touch that —"

What happened next was straight out of Mr. Bing's patent application. *Flack!* The U-Bundle mechanism launched a length of twine out past the target. It boomeranged and wrapped itself three times around the bush. Small teeth on the end of the rope bit in tightly, cinching the cord. A split second later, *Whack!* The Safe-chete blade knifed out and sliced through the honeysuckle branches. The neat bundle tipped over and landed at Darren's feet.

"Whoa!" said Darren, surprised and impressed. "Check it out!"

Barefoot, Griffin sailed down the stairs and out of the house, struggling to be quiet in his fury. He hit the grass running, and made a beeline for Darren.

Big Darren Vader was not normally intimidated by the smaller Griffin. But the blind rage could be felt from a range of thirty yards. He turned tail and fled, though weighed down by the heavy equipment.

Flack! Whack!

Suddenly, an escape route appeared in the hedge separating the Bing home from their neighbors. Darren disappeared through the opening. Hot on his heels, Griffin tripped over the neatly bundled cedar shrubs, ripping open both knees of his pajama pants. Then he was up again, pounding across the neighbors' yard, fueled by white-hot anger.

Flack! Whack!

A perfectly pruned rosebush was cinched and slashed, all in the blink of an eye.

"Stop doing that!" Griffin seethed.

"It's not my fault these controls are so sensitive!" Darren shot back. The Safe-chete blade beheaded a petunia.

Griffin made a lunge for the back of the SweetPick's harness, but Darren sidestepped. A lasso of twine snapped past Griffin's ear.

Darren was still defiant. "I feel sorry for you, Bing. If my folks bet our future on a NosePick, I wouldn't show my face around town."

"It's a *Sweet*Pick!"

Darren beat a hasty retreat for the road. Griffin was determined not to let him off so easily. He was going to show his father, and also Mrs. Vader, how Darren was treating a top secret prototype like it was a sandbox toy. The SweetPick had been entrusted to Mrs. Vader in good faith. If this was how she looked after it, Dad should think about getting another lawyer.

Despite his reduced speed, Darren was hard to catch up to. He played middle school football, and ran with a high-stepping gait that covered a lot of ground.

Fine, thought Griffin. *I'll beat him at his own game.* He threw himself at Darren's legs in a flying tackle. One arm found its target around Darren's knees. The other found the dangling button that operated the SweetPick.

Flack! Thud!

The Safe-chete mechanism burst out and lodged itself in the trunk of a large sycamore tree.

Griffin knew a new panic. "Pull it out!"

Darren yanked with all his might, but the blade was truly stuck. He turned to Griffin. "You are so dead!"

"Me?! You're the one who stole it!"

Darren nodded solemnly. "Yeah, but you're the one who broke it."

"I wouldn't even be here if you hadn't woken me up! I'd be safe in my bed having a really good dream!"

"Well, maybe if your dad invented something normal for a change, I'd be able to resist making fun of it!"

It was the last straw. With a howl of outrage, Griffin clamped his arms around Darren and wrestled him to the ground. With a deep *thwang*, the Safe-chete blade was dislodged from the trunk. The two boys stopped fighting and stared at it.

"Let's get this back in my garage before our parents kill us!" Darren blurted.

"Right!" Griffin agreed.

It rankled to have to help Darren cover this up when the whole thing was the jerk's fault to begin with. Yet Griffin forced himself to focus on the big picture. It would be satisfying to see Darren get in trouble. But keeping the SweetPick a secret was far more important, at least until it was patented. So he accompanied Darren back to the Vader house and helped his enemy stow the prototype under a tarpaulin in the garage. He even nodded when Darren said, "Tonight never happened. Got it, Bing?"

Then he padded home, still barefoot, pajamas ripped in the knees. *Anyway*, he reflected, *there would be plenty of opportunities to take revenge on Darren.* It would be easy for The Man With The Plan.

The next morning, Griffin answered the knock on his bedroom door to find his father standing in the hall.

"Hi, Dad. What's up?"

"My blood pressure, mostly," his father replied gravely. "Old man Abernathy paid us a visit bright and early this morning. Have you got an explanation for this?" He held up a bundled rosebush, its dead blooms dropping petals on the carpet.

Griffin's heart sank. He had been hoping the cranky neighbor would swallow his loss and keep quiet about it. Then all that would need explaining was the hole in the hedge. Maybe he could convince Dad he'd done it himself in his early SweetPick testing.

No such luck.

"Did the SweetPick do that?" Griffin asked innocently.

"Yes and no," replied Mr. Bing. "A SweetPick can't do anything on its own. So I'll ask you again. Have

8

you got an explanation for this? Did you take the SweetPick out for a test run before I handed it over to Mrs. Vader?"

Griffin made a face. He didn't want to be a rat, even though the person he'd be ratting out was his worst enemy, who had totally brought this on himself. He also didn't want to lie to his father. Fine. He'd throw Darren to the wolves.

But before he could open his mouth, his father went on. "It's been rough since the patent office turned me down. I don't know what I'd do without Mrs. Vader to guide me through the reapplication process."

And there, just about to drive Darren straight to jail, Griffin had to jam on the brakes and change direction again. If Dad found out that Mrs. Vader couldn't control her own son and keep his mitts off the prototype, it would destroy his faith in the lawyer that he needed so badly. That put Griffin in a position he would have considered unthinkable.

I have to lie to protect Darren!

"It was me," he confessed, shamefaced. "Like you said, I did it before you sent the SweetPick to Mrs. Vader, and I stood the bundles up, hoping nobody would notice."

His father was exasperated. "Are you kidding? Abernathy notices which direction every blade of grass is supposed to be pointing!"

Griffin studied his sneakers. "I'm really, really sorry, Dad. I didn't want to tell you because you were already so upset about the patent thing."

The lecture was loud and long, and the bitterest part was that Griffin didn't deserve any of it. The only thing he himself was guilty of was catapulting the Safe-chete blade into that tree.

If he expected to get any special appreciation from Darren for taking this rap, he was sadly mistaken.

"You are some loser, Bing," Vader said when Griffin confronted him at lunch that day. "I mean, I've heard of lying to get out of trouble, but to lie to get *into* it — that's a special kind of stupid!"

"You're welcome," Griffin seethed. "You know, for saving your neck at the cost of my own."

"What do you want — a medal, or just a hero cookie? Now beat it. I'm savoring the moment."

The worst part was that Darren would never understand why Griffin was covering for him. Darren's parents were both successful attorneys. He didn't know what it was to watch your father struggle.

Someday, Vader. Someday when you least expect it . . .

GIGA-PRIZE SET TO EXPIRE OCTOBER 6

It's the stuff dreams are made of. Last October, someone on Long Island purchased a Giga-Millions lottery ticket with the numbers 12, 17, 18, 34, 37, and 55. And, when those numbers all came up on lottery night, the ticket was worth $29,876,454.53.

A fairy tale, right?

Not exactly.

The owner of the ticket has never come forward. By law, lottery winners have only one year to claim their prize. After that, the ticket becomes worthless, and the money goes back into the lottery pool. That's what will happen to this thirty-million-dollar payday when the lottery office closes at 6:00 p.m. on October 6, three weeks from today.

So what's the deal here? It's easy to imagine a person buying a lottery ticket and forgetting about it, tossing it into the garbage along with old gas receipts and expired grocery coupons. Or perhaps we're dealing with a crafty new millionaire who's planning to wait till the last minute to redeem his windfall in the national media spotlight. Then there's the possibility of a story-book ending — that somewhere out there is a Giga-Millionaire who simply doesn't know it.

As the deadline approaches, a lot of Long Islanders will be checking their wallets, their purses, their pockets, and their junk drawers in the hope of finding that lost ticket to the Good Life.

Ben Slovak put the newspaper down on the cafeteria table. "You want to hear the kicker? They know the ticket was bought at the convenience store by the train station in Green Hollow. That's the next town past Cedarville! My dad gets coffee there on his way to work."

"Maybe you're rich and you don't even know it," Griffin suggested.

"Fat chance." Ben broke off a piece of turkey from his sandwich and held it inside his collar. A small, furry, needle-nosed snout came up and grabbed it — belonging to Ferret Face, the ferret Ben carried at all times under his shirt for medical purposes. "My father doesn't believe in lotteries. He says it's like flushing money down the toilet. The odds are astronomical."

"It wasn't astronomical for the guy with the right numbers," Pitch Benson pointed out. "Man, thirty million bucks! I'd take my whole family to climb Mount Everest! The mountain permits alone are, like, a hundred grand each."

Melissa Dukakis agitated her head, parting the curtain of stringy hair that normally obscured her face. "Think of the computing power thirty million would buy! I'd be invincible!"

"You're invincible now," Ben reminded her. "Who's better at tech stuff than you?"

"I'm good," she conceded modestly. "Just not invincible."

Logan Kellerman sighed wanly. "If I had that kind of money, I wouldn't waste it on dumb stuff like that. I'd produce a movie, and cast myself in the lead role."

"Good thing you wouldn't waste it on dumb stuff," Pitch said sarcastically.

Savannah looked disgusted. "You guys are so self-ish. Big money like that — sure, you keep a little for yourself. But there's only one thing to do with that kind of fortune — help others."

"Well, you're a better person than me," put in Ben. "It takes a big heart to want to do things for people."

"Who said anything about people?" Savannah demanded, outraged. "People can take care of themselves. I'd do things for animals."

It got a big laugh around the lunch table. Savannah was legendary as Cedarville's number one animal lover. Besides her dog, Luthor, she was the housemate — never say *owner* — of a menagerie that included a capuchin monkey, rabbits (numbers varied), hamsters (ditto), a pack rat, and an albino chameleon named Lorenzo.

Griffin looked unhappy. "It's great to give money to people, or animals, or charities. But I don't think it's so selfish to want a little extra cash for your family. It doesn't have to be the whole thirty mil. But it would be nice to have something to fall back on if my dad's latest invention turns out to be a bust." The stress showing in his face, he told the others how the patent office had rejected the first application for the SweetPick.

"Don't worry," Ben said soothingly. "Your father's inventions always seem totally useless at first, but they usually work out in the end."

"Tell that to Vader." Griffin was bitter. "He stole the SweetPick prototype and woke me up last week. Crunch-'n'-munched half the landscape. I got keel-hauled by my dad and took all the blame for something Vader did."

"Darren's such a jerk," Savannah commiserated.

They all looked across the cafeteria to where Darren sat in solitary splendor, his mouth open wide enough to drive a truck through, about to tie into a gigantic hero sandwich.

"I'm kind of amazed he's at school today at all," Ben said. "I thought he'd be out there scouring the streets with a magnifying glass, looking for that lottery ticket."

"He probably hasn't heard about it yet," Pitch muttered. "Vader would trade his own mother for a free Happy Meal. Imagine what he'd do for thirty million bucks! The minute he reads this article, believe me, the search will be on."

"No way," Ben scoffed. "That ticket's a year old already. It's probably mush down some sewer, or smoke up an incinerator chimney. Even Darren's not crazy enough to go looking for it."

"Yeah, probably not," Griffin agreed. All at once, a familiar expression appeared on the face of The Man With The Plan. "Unless he has a little help . . ."

"Hold on there, cowboy," Pitch said darkly. "I know the beginnings of a plan when I see one. And I'm looking at one right now."

Griffin glanced around the table. "Every single one of us has been victimized at one time or another by Darren Vader. Wouldn't it be great to get back at him?"

Ben regarded him suspiciously, and even Ferret

Face poked his beady eyes out to have a peek. "I don't know. Would it?"

"Of course!" Griffin exclaimed. "We're not going to hurt him. We just need to knock him down a couple of pegs, show the world what a money-grubbing creep he is. Who's with me?"

"Oh, me," said Melissa instantly.

Pitch was skeptical. "Let me get this straight. Vader insulted your dad's sugar slicer, so we all have to sign on to prove to the world that he's greedy?"

"Look," said Griffin, "I was the victim this time. But Darren has gotten all of us over the years." He looked from face to face. "Ben — how many times has he called you a shrimp? Logan — he makes fun of your acting! Pitch — he's as much your worst enemy as mine! Savannah — he's mean to Luthor!"

"Okay," Savannah assented. "For Luthor."

In the end, they were all in, as Griffin knew they would be. He may not have won the Nobel Prize in Planning, but his team was second to none, and loyal to the end.

"Welcome to Operation Treasure Hunt," he proclaimed.

Melissa's room looked like the IT center of a large corporation. Just standing on the rug, you could feel your back teeth vibrating from the power hum of so many computers and other electronic devices.

Griffin, Ben, and Melissa watched breathlessly as the page came out of the printer.

"Why is it gray like that?" Ben asked, frowning.

"I used the same stock of newsprint as the *Cedarville Herald*," Melissa explained. "It's supposed to look like a real newspaper clipping, right?"

Griffin picked up the page. "It's perfect," he decided aloud. "Better than perfect. You even put part of an ad for bananas on the back."

Melissa's pink face emerged from her hair to acknowledge this praise. "Plantains, actually. But, yeah, I thought it would be a nice touch." She took a pair of scissors and snipped out the "article." When she was done, all three were satisfied that it was indistinguishable from an actual newspaper clipping.

LOCAL WOMAN TOSSES MILLIONS

A Cedarville woman had thirty million dollars in the palm of her hand yesterday — until she threw it away. The woman, who asked that her name be withheld, became swept up in the lottery fever that has taken hold of Long Island ever since it was revealed that a Giga-Millions jackpot still remained unclaimed. She found the ticket in a jacket that had been misplaced by the cleaners for about eight months, and set it aside to be taken to the lottery office. The woman, who is ninety-two and suffers from short-term memory problems, was unable to find the ticket when her son came to drive her to cash it in. The two have been tearing the house and the trash apart since yesterday morning, with no luck.

"It must have gone out with the garbage," she said sadly. "It was an honest mistake."

An honest mistake, yes. But a very expensive one.

"It's gorgeous," Ben admitted. "But are you sure it's obvious enough? Maybe we should add another line about how, if you go through every trash can in town, you'll probably find it."

"Don't worry," Griffin assured him. "If anyone can connect the dots, Vader can. The guy thinks about money twenty-four seven. If he believes there's thirty mil out there for the taking, he won't rest until he's crawled around every Dumpster east of the Queens line!"

Ben took Ferret Face from his shirt and encouraged the little creature to walk across the clipping, making tiny claw holes and wet spots from his cold moist nose. "You know, to give it the 'broken-in' look, like people have been handling it."

Melissa had a practical question. "How are we going to make sure Darren sees it?"

"The easy way." Griffin grinned. "We'll tell him he can't see it. Then he'll see it, or die trying."

It was a role without lines, but Logan was ready to throw himself into it anyway. A true actor could communicate more with a gesture, a frown, or a smile than most people could with a two-hour speech. The great Stanislavski said that — or was it Marcel Marceau?

He glanced up at Pitch, the lookout. The climber had taken her position in the oak tree by the school's side entrance, where Logan sat on the tarmac, his back leaning against the wall. The signal was a birdcall, but unfortunately, there were actual birds in that tree, too. Logan had already suffered four false alarms. No matter. An actor was always ready to think on his feet.

The next time he heard the whistle, he looked up to read Pitch's lips — he couldn't do that with the birds since he didn't read beaks. It was the real thing this time. He took out the newspaper clipping and began to study it.

A moment later, Darren lumbered around the side of the building.

Getting into character, Logan looked startled, folded up the paper, and jammed it into his pocket.

"Hey, Kellerman, what've you got there?"

Logan just shook his head. He got to his feet and started away, looking furtive.

Darren caught up with him in three strides. "I asked you a question. What were you reading?"

In answer, Logan began to walk faster.

The much larger Darren grabbed him by the collar, spun him around, and reached into his pocket. Logan struggled, but was soon overpowered. The bigger boy pulled out the phony clipping.

"A pleasure doing business with you, loser." Darren started off, unfolding the paper.

Logan caught a glimpse of Pitch in the tree, shooting him a thumbs-up. Good reviews already. Very satisfying.

The first sign that Operation Treasure Hunt was working came when Darren didn't show up for school the next morning.

"Does anyone know where Darren is?" asked Mrs. Selznick, their homeroom teacher.

"Maybe he's sick," Griffin piped up helpfully.

The team knew better, of course. Darren was out Dumpster-diving in the hope of coming up with a thirty-million-dollar ticket. It was the plan in all its glory, playing out exactly the way Griffin had designed it.

Ben could see the triumphant smile on his best friend's face. And Ben was smiling, too. Sort of. When an operation was in progress, there was always an underlying feeling of nervousness and even dread. Ferret Face felt it, too. He was scrambling around under Ben's sweatshirt, unable to get comfortable, his claws pinching at his owner's chest. Normally, the little ferret was supposed to leave the skin alone unless he sensed that Ben was falling asleep. Ben suffered from narcolepsy, and sometimes dozed off in the middle of the day. It was Ferret Face's job to keep him awake and alert by delivering a wake-up nip at the right moment.

"This is a very good day," Griffin whispered as Mrs. Selznick began the lesson.

Ben nodded, and stifled his unease. It was a feeling you had to get used to if you were going to be best friends with The Man With The Plan. And as plans went, Operation Treasure Hunt was a lot less risky than most.

The first Darren sighting came at noon when the big boy showed up in the cafeteria.

"Figures," muttered Pitch. "He blows off all his morning classes, but when it comes time to feed his face, he's a diligent student."

Darren's rat's nest of hair was even wilder than usual, and Ben was pretty sure he could see a few eggshell fragments amid the unruly curls. His clothes were rumpled, too, and there was a big smear of something dark across his forehead. In addition, he didn't seem to notice the orange peel hanging out of his hip pocket.

"I don't know," Savannah observed critically. "I was kind of hoping that he'd look — you know — worse."

Then Darren tried to select a seat. There was a loud chorus of "Pee-yew!" and every single person at that table got up and moved as far away as possible.

Griffin was triumphant. "I think he *smells* worse."

As they made their way to their table, Griffin sidled by his enemy. "Thought you were sick today."

"Thought you knew how to mind your own business," came a growled reply.

Griffin shrugged. "Nice cologne, by the way. What is it — eau de swamp gas?"

OPERATION Treasure Hunt – Plan Checklist

Garbage smell	X
Fruit rind on person	X
Coating of vacuum cleaner fuzz	X
Unidentified smear	X
Tomato sauce staining socks	X
Flies	X
Eggshells in hair	(unconfirmed – possible dandruff)

Every day after school, Griffin and Ben rode around town on their bikes, looking for the site of Darren's current excavation. They always found him, waist-deep in refuse, searching, ever searching. His rubber gloves were practically shredded by the hundreds of twist ties he'd undone. Whenever the clank of trash can lids could be heard, Darren was not far away. The big boy had learned to hoist himself into a Dumpster with the athletic grace of an Olympic pole-vaulter.

He sifted through coffee grounds, apple cores, and old congealed spaghetti. He fought with caterpillars, pigeons, and angry raccoons. Any small slip of paper was pounced on. Was this the thirty-million-dollar ticket? Bitter disappointment followed as he encountered yet another business card, or laundry list, or Post-it note, or cash register receipt. Worst of all was finding an actual ticket and checking the date and numbers only to discover that it was the wrong one. Again.

"You know what?" Ben ventured on day three. "I think we should tell him. He's suffered enough."

"Are you kidding me?" Griffin retorted. "He could suffer for ten more lifetimes, and it wouldn't be enough!"

So Ben held his peace. There was no sense arguing with Griffin when a plan was in progress.

They were on their way home that afternoon when they looked down Ninth Street and spied a man in his twenties diligently sifting through the contents of a garbage can.

Ben was mystified. "That's not Darren."

"Relax," Griffin said soothingly. "You worry too

much. The guy probably lost his wedding ring or something."

But a few blocks later, it happened again. This time it was a mother and a daughter ransacking the trash can at the corner of Honeybee Street.

Alarm bells went off in Ben's head. "You don't think people are finding out about this? You know — seeing Darren in the garbage, and putting two and two together?"

Griffin frowned. "That isn't part of the plan."

"Never mind the plan! What are we going to do if the word gets out that there's a thirty-million-dollar payday just lying there somewhere in Cedarville? The whole world could show up here to dig through our trash!"

The next day, Griffin and Ben passed no fewer than six garbage hunters on the way to school.

The other team members were waiting for them at their lockers.

"I've got a bad feeling about this," Savannah proclaimed darkly. "A guy was going through our trash bags last night. Luthor had to chase him away. You know it's not good for Luthor to return to his old guard-dog self."

"My mom thinks we have raccoons," Logan put in. "Our garbage was all over the place this morning."

"What's going on, Griffin?" Pitch added. "How did all these other people get sucked into Operation Treasure Hunt?"

Griffin shrugged. "It's just bad luck. Somebody saw Darren and figured out what he was up to. Everybody knows about the missing ticket."

Shy Melissa peered out from behind her hair. "Do you think maybe we should tell Darren it's all a hoax?"

"Absolutely not," Griffin said firmly. "The only thing worse than regular Darren is blackmailer Darren. He'll hold it over our heads forever. It'll cost us our lunch money from now until the end of college, and mortgage payments after that!"

TOURISTS FLOCKING TO CEDARVILLE?
TRY GARBAGE PICKERS

If you've looked out the window lately, you've surely noticed a lot of fresh faces around town. No, they're not here to visit downtown shops and restaurants, or our world-class waterfront and marina. They're here to go through the garbage.

A rumor has spread that the missing Giga-Millions lottery ticket that is due to expire in less than three weeks has been tossed in the trash somewhere here in Cedarville. People are coming from far and wide to join the hunt. So far, the result has been garbage-strewn streets, odor problems, traffic conges-tion, and a 200 percent increase in rodent sightings.

Also, the Cedarville Police Department reports danger-ous sanitary conditions in and around the municipal dump as the searchers trace the miss-ing ticket to the next logical step, from sidewalk to general disposal.

The source of this trouble-some rumor is a mystery, but the police are treating it as mali-cious mischief.

"I suppose some folks might consider this a joke," said Detective Sergeant Vizzini of the Cedarville PD. "But when you

Malicious mischief," Logan repeated. "That sounds bad. Something like that could get me blacklisted in Hollywood."

"My mother can't stop talking about this," Ben added worriedly. "I mean, she can't stop talking about anything, but this has turned into her favorite subject! She got a parking violation on Main Street. And before she could pay it, some guy stole it! It's like no piece of paper is safe in this town!"

Griffin tried to look unruffled. "I'll bet the competition is driving Vader crazy. He's probably up all night worrying that somebody will find the ticket before he does."

"My *dad's* the competition!" Pitch complained. "He's leaving work early to come home and sort through filth! And I can't even tell him he's wasting his time, because how could I explain why I know?"

"It's getting away from us, Griffin," Savannah added. "That's a real newspaper talking about real cops."

Griffin nodded. "I admit that I never expected it to go this far. But it's bound to blow over. You have to have faith in the plan. No matter what happens, there's absolutely no way anybody could trace it to us."

*　*　*

It was the kind of situation they didn't prepare you for at the police academy. The mid-September weather was hot, and the Cedarville municipal dump was plenty ripe. Handkerchiefs over their noses, Detective Sergeant Vizzini and his fellow officers marched thirty-three would-be millionaires down the mountain of refuse to a line of police vehicles.

The interviews were pungent, short, and extremely belligerent. The interviewees all truly believed that the winning ticket might very well lie under the next moldy watermelon rind.

"What would you say," asked Vizzini, "if I told you that there's no evidence whatsoever that that ticket still exists anywhere, let alone in this town?"

"I'd say you're trying to put me off the scent so you can keep the money for yourself!" shrilled an angry woman.

"Well, exactly how did you come to the conclusion that the ticket was out here somewhere?" the detective persisted.

"Everybody knows that! It's all over town!"

His policeman's instincts told him that was the key. How had the rumor gotten its start? Most searchers told a similar story — that they had seen others searching and thought they'd try their hand, too. But someone had to have been first. He listened to endless tales of voices heard in Dumpsters, and strangers peering into trash cans and slicing open green plastic bags. Through it all, a theme began to emerge:

".. . and then I saw that kid . . ."

".. . a thirteen-year-old boy climbed out of the bin . . ."

".. . big kid, probably in middle school . . ."

Vizzini's eyes narrowed. In his career as an officer of the peace in Cedarville, he had learned that it was never a waste to follow up on a lead that began with "that kid."

"What kid?" he asked pointedly.

"You know, the son of those two lawyers. The Vader kid."

Half an hour later, at the Vader home, Darren cracked almost immediately. "It's no fair! I knew the ticket was in Cedarville before all those guys copied me! If they win the money, I should at least get half!"

"But how did you learn that the ticket was in Cedarville?" Vizzini pressed.

"From the newspaper article," Darren replied.

"What newspaper article?"

Hands trembling, the boy pulled a tattered clipping out of his pocket and unfolded it.

It took a short telephone call to the *Cedarville Herald* to confirm that the article was a fake.

"All right, Darren," Mrs. Vader told her son. "You're not in any trouble, but you have to tell the detective where you found that clipping."

"I stole it off of — uh — Logan Kellerman gave it to me!"

From there the investigation proceeded quickly — from the Kellerman house, to the Dukakis house, to the home of one Griffin Bing.

L uthor picked up a blackened banana peel, dangling it delicately from huge canine teeth, and dropped it into Savannah's bag.

"Thanks, sweetie," she said with a sigh, patting his huge Doberman head.

Pitch hefted a shovelful of moldy bread and directed it into her own sack. "You know, people are disgusting. I get that they thought there was thirty million bucks to be had, but that's still no excuse for being a slob!"

The team was fanned out across Ninth Street, serving day one of their sentence of community service. Luckily, Detective Sergeant Vizzini had decided not to press charges for the malicious mischief of the lottery hoax. Instead, the friends were assigned to clean up Cedarville. The fortune hunters were all gone now, but in their wake they had left a foul-smelling debris field of overturned cans and torn plastic bags.

"Hey, get back here!" Ben dropped his broom and took off across the garbage-strewn sidewalk in pursuit of Ferret Face. The little creature dove under a pile of newspapers and came out with a half-eaten hot dog. Ben snatched it away. "No chance, buster! You don't know where that's been!"

"He knows exactly where it's been, and so do you," Griffin pointed out. "It's been in the garbage. It *is* the garbage!"

"No offense, Griffin, but stuff a sock in it," muttered Logan. "I ought to have my head examined for following you and your cockamamie plans. It's only a short step from community service to community theater. My talent belongs to the world, not some podunk playhouse."

There was a chorus of discontented mumbling from the entire team.

"Come on, you guys," Griffin reproached them. "We've gotten blowback from operations before this."

"We've gotten blowback from operations that were *necessary*," Pitch amended. "This was just to make Darren look like a clown — which is something he does pretty well on his own, with or without our help!"

A squad car drove by on Ninth Street, the officer looking at them pointedly as he passed. The workers went back to their jobs.

Savannah heaved a sigh. "Well, at least things can finally calm down around here now that everybody knows the lottery ticket was a hoax."

Melissa stopped sweeping, her eyes peeking out from behind her hair. "That's not technically true.

What we did to Darren was a hoax. But the missing ticket — whatever happened to it — is a *fact*."

"Thanks for that, Melissa," Ben groaned. "When I'm wading through garbage, nothing cheers me up like thinking about money I'm never going to have."

An SUV pulled up to the curb. The window whispered down, and Mrs. Benson leaned out. "Get in, Pitch, and make sure you sit on the plastic."

"Sergeant Vizzini said we have to stay till five."

"I've already informed the police." Pitch's mother looked disgusted. "What fun — having to clear my daughter's dentist appointment with the law!" Her jaundiced eye found Griffin. "Pitch was never in trouble a day in her life until she started palling around with you. If I had my way, that would come to an end."

"Mom, don't be so dramatic," Pitch put in tiredly.

"And she was certainly never a bully," Mrs. Benson went on, as if no one had spoken. "You ought to be ashamed of yourself for the way you bullied that poor Vader boy!"

Griffin was shocked. "I didn't bully Darren, Mrs. Benson."

"Well, I don't know what else you'd call it, sending the poor boy crawling through garbage and humiliating him in front of the whole town!"

Pitch shot Griffin a small shrug as they drove off.

Griffin was horrified. "Can you believe that? Me, bullying Vader? If you look up 'bully' in the dictionary, there's a picture of him!"

"Listen, Griffin," Ben said, "*we* know that because we've been dealing with Darren our whole lives. But think what it looks like to the adults in this town. We weren't fighting for justice or saving animals this time. To anybody who doesn't know Vader, this was a hundred percent mean."

Griffin found no comfort at home, either. His parents understood all too well that their son was The Man With The Plan. Whatever had happened, it was a sure bet that Griffin was the ringleader.

"I know you don't like Darren Vader very much," his mother said primly. "But that's no excuse for making a fool of the poor boy."

"First that stunt with the SweetPick, and now this," his father added. "Griffin, you've got to get your head on straight."

That was the worst part of all. He'd already lied to keep Darren's name out of the SweetPick incident. How could he tell the truth now and expect to be believed? But he'd only taken the rap in the first place so Dad wouldn't have a beef with Mrs. Vader, who he depended on for business. It was so unfair!

Nor was there any relief for Griffin at school. The story of the lottery hoax was all over town, driven by gossip and the fact that the streets were littered with torn garbage bags and trash. On Monday, Dr. Egan, the principal, called for a schoolwide anti-bullying assembly. Griffin could feel dozens of eyes burning into his flesh as speeches were made and videos shown. It was one of the most uncomfortable hours of his life.

Finally, just as the torture appeared to be coming to an end, a hand shot up near the front.

"Dr. Egan," came an all-too-familiar voice. "May I please say a few words to everybody?" Darren Vader stood up, his face radiating sincerity.

How could the principal say no? This was the boy the whole town knew had been the victim of exactly what the assembly was about.

Darren joined Dr. Egan onstage and accepted the microphone. "It isn't easy for me to talk about this. I still feel hurt and embarrassed, but — *I* was bullied."

Griffin recoiled in horror. Darren was looking directly at him.

"I haven't been sleeping so great since it happened, so I've had a lot of time to think about it. I've figured out that the only way to get past my pain is to forgive the people who did this to me. And so I do. All except one — the one who thought it up, The Man With The — well, let's just say that the whole thing was his idea."

Well, that does it, Griffin thought in agony. That last part was as good as a giant neon sign that said: THERE HE IS! THE BIG, BAD BULLY! Now the entire school was staring at him. Even his team looked kind of dis-approving, all except Melissa. And he couldn't be sure about her, because it was impossible to get a look at her whole face. Only Ben seemed a little sympathetic — surely you could expect support from your best friend!

But Ferret Face must have sensed the scorn of the crowd, because his beady eyes were cold and glaring.

Dr. Egan hurriedly snatched back the microphone. "Well, thank you, Darren, for those — uh — inspiring words. Let's remember what was said here this morning. We'll dismiss from the rear."

On the way back to homeroom through the crowded halls, Logan caught up to the others. "Man, did you hear that? Darren must have been really hurt!"

"Are you kidding me?" Griffin was beyond annoyed. "How can you call yourself an actor when you just fell for the biggest acting job since they paved Broadway? You want to talk about bullying? How about standing up in front of eight hundred kids and telling them to be mad at one person? It's got to be the first time in history that there was bullying onstage in the middle of an anti-bullying assembly!"

"Hey, you guys, wait up!" A short, slight, blue-eyed boy with blond hair spiked on top fell into step with them. "Can I walk with you? This school's totally confusing. I couldn't find my homeroom with a GPS."

Pitch laughed. "Just pick a direction, then go the opposite way. It usually ends up right."

Victor Phoenix had arrived in Cedarville the previous week at the height of the Dumpster-diving frenzy. On his first day at school, he'd had his new classmates howling with laughter at his description of moving day.

"We unpacked our stuff. But as soon as we put the boxes at the curb, these people came and tore everything apart! It was like a snowstorm out there! I was positive we'd moved to the Twilight Zone!"

"I guess your Twilight Zone theory just got confirmed," Griffin told him now. "Did you catch that act in there with Darren Vader?"

Victor's response was dead serious. "It took a lot of courage to speak up the way he did."

Griffin bit his tongue. The kid was new, which meant he hadn't had a chance to get to know Vader yet.

He'd learn soon enough.

That afternoon's community service brought the cleanup crew to Ravine Road, on the outskirts of downtown. Luckily, the Nassau County street sweepers had been through this area, so there wasn't much to do beyond rebagging the wire trash bins and a little light cleaning with their brooms. After about twenty minutes of work, they were done.

"Maybe we should move on to the next block," Melissa suggested in her quiet voice.

There was a chorus of groans, all in the negative.

"Do I look like a garbage-picking wizard?" Ben demanded. "I clean what I have to, and nothing more."

Pitch checked her climber's watch. "We're still on the clock for the next forty minutes."

Luthor suddenly stiffened, his cropped ears at attention. A low growl rose in his mighty throat. A few seconds later, a light-furred Siamese cat trotted around the corner, tail held high. The big Doberman emitted a sound that would not have been out of place coming from a *T. rex*. He was off like a shot.

"Luthor!" exclaimed Savannah harshly.

Terrified, the little Siamese whipped back around the corner, out of sight. A moment later, she reappeared in the arms of none other than Victor Phoenix.

"Oh, hey, you guys," the newcomer called. "Street's looking good."

"We lucked out this time," Pitch explained. "The sweeper truck got here first."

Savannah could see only the cat. "Oh, she's gorgeous! Look at those blue eyes! Is she a real applehead Siamese?"

Victor nodded. "Wow, you sure know a lot about cats."

Griffin laughed. "Also dogs, ocelots, boll weevils, lions, koalas, and Komodo dragons."

Victor shot him a *Who asked you?* look, and then turned back to Savannah. "Her name is Penelope. I've had her since she was a kitten." His face turned tragic. "But I don't think I'll have her much longer."

Savannah looked alarmed. "Is she sick?"

"No, but my dad is. He's developed a sudden allergy to cat dander. The doctor says it must have been triggered by the move — you know, the cat hair flying when we packed up all our stuff."

Savannah reached out and plucked Penelope from his arms. "Oh, sweetie," she cooed. "So soft! Our two cats are senior citizens. They have wisdom, but I'd forgotten how much fun the young ones can be."

Luthor tried to insert his enormous head between Savannah and the cat she held. In his mind, *he* was "sweetie."

Savannah pushed him away. "Not now."

But a nanosecond later, Luthor was back, trying to lick Savannah's face.

"I think someone might be jealous," Ben commented.

"Don't be silly," Savannah said, absently scratching behind Penelope's silky ears. "Luthor's never jealous. We live with lots of animals, including cats. We're one big happy family."

Victor reached out and took his cat back. "You're lucky. All I have is Penelope. And tomorrow I have to take her to the animal shelter."

"No, you don't," Savannah said firmly. "Bring Penelope to my house instead."

"But, Savannah!" Griffin gasped. "Your mom said she'd disown you if you brought home another pet!"

Victor scorched him with a look that would have melted lead.

Griffin recoiled. *What did I ever do to that guy?*

"First of all," Savannah lectured, "they're not pets. They're friends, equals. And second, we're not adopting her. We're just taking her until Victor's dad works out his allergy problem."

Victor was overcome. "You would do that for *me*? You hardly know me!"

"It's no big deal," she assured him. "Penelope will live at my house while you get your dad a good doctor. Obviously, you're welcome to come and visit her as often as you want."

"And you're sure it'll be okay with your folks?"

"Absolutely."

Luthor watched in dismay as the cat was handed back to Savannah. His short cropped tail abruptly stopped wagging.

On Wednesday, Griffin set his tray down at the long cafeteria table to find Logan and Victor poring over a large cardboard chart, so absorbed that their lunches sat ignored.

"What's that?" Griffin asked.

"It's our Oscar prediction chart," Logan explained. "See? We've got all the major award categories on the board, and the possible nominees on Post-it notes. When new movies come out, we make our best guess about which actors and directors and writers and so on have a chance at which awards. Like, for best actor —" He stared at Victor. "Christian Bale? No way! What about Johnny Depp?"

Victor pointed to a Post-it on the other side. "I have him down for supporting actor in that cowboy flick."

Logan's eyes became dreamy. "I could have *killed* in that role."

"You're an actor?" Victor asked.

"Are you kidding? Remember that commercial for Toenail Fungus Genie? I was the kid who said, 'Works on jock itch, too.' "

Victor looked impressed. "That was you?"

Savannah sat down next to them. "Hi, Griffin. What's up?"

"I'm being totally ignored like I don't even exist," Griffin informed her conversationally.

"Cool," she said absently. "Hey, Victor, I shot some video of Penelope playing with Cleopatra, my monkey." She slid her phone across the table.

Griffin took a bite of his sandwich, only to find his appetite gone.

Melissa arrived, and handed Victor a flash drive containing a special debugging program for his computer. Pitch was next, bearing a length of climbing rope and a carabiner. She and Victor began showing each other various knots.

Griffin couldn't help himself. "He's a climber, too?"

"No," said Pitch, barely looking up. "An Eagle Scout."

Griffin looked on in amazement. Victor Phoenix had barely been in town a week, and already it was like he'd been friends with everybody since kindergarten.

Ben was the last to join them. He sat down and began to tie into his lunch.

Good old Ben, Griffin thought. At least he could rely on his best friend not to have forged a deep personal connection with the new guy.

Ben tore off a piece of bologna and handed it down his collar. All at once, he began to squirm, scratching madly under his T-shirt.

"What's the matter with you?" asked Savannah.

"Ferret Face is shedding," said Ben in a strangled voice, continuing to wriggle. "His fur is inside all my clothes! The itch is driving me crazy!"

Victor looked up from the rope. "You ought to try mixing a raw egg in with his chopped meat," he advised thoughtfully. "It'll stop that shedding, and egg will make his coat shiny, too."

Ben beamed. "Thanks a lot! I'm ready to try anything at this point."

Did this kid have an answer for everything? Griffin decided to give it a try. "You know, Victor, my foot's been bugging me lately. The back of my shoe's been rubbing against my ankle."

"So?" Victor returned to his knot tying with Pitch.

"So have you got any advice for me?"

Victor shrugged coldly. "Do I look like a shoemaker?"

Griffin looked around the table. Melissa and Ben were eating; Savannah was watching cat and monkey videos; Logan was rearranging his Oscar picks; and Pitch was affixing an elaborate knot to her carabiner. No one had been paying attention when Victor dissed him so totally.

Why does Victor Phoenix hate me?

After lunch, Victor left early to head to the locker

room for gym. The others were about to go their separate ways when Griffin called the table to order.

"Make it fast," requested Logan, rolling up his Oscar chart and securing it with a rubber band. "I want to get this stowed before I forget Victor's locker combination."

"Guys," said Griffin urgently, "don't you notice something a little weird about Victor?"

"He's nice," offered Melissa timidly.

"Don't you think it's a bit of a coincidence that he just so happens to be interested in exactly the things you guys are interested in? He loves movies . . . and cats; he's good with a computer; he ties knots; he knows how to keep a ferret from shedding. Doesn't that set off any alarm bells?"

Ben shrugged. "He's smart. He knows about a lot of different things. I like him."

"I know you think the main basis for a friendship is getting your friends arrested," Pitch added. "But in the real world, people hit it off because they have stuff in common."

"Okay, how about this, then," Griffin persisted. "Have you noticed that he hates my guts?"

"Don't be paranoid," Savannah scoffed. "He doesn't hate anybody's guts."

"He hates mine!" Griffin's voice was rising. "He ignores me like I'm not even here. And when he does talk to me, it's only to say something nasty. He's worse than Vader."

"Oh, come on!" Ben scoffed. "How do you compare any human with Vader?"

"I'm serious," Griffin insisted. "With Darren, at least you know where you stand — he hates everybody."

"You're imagining things," Ben accused. "You know why we like Victor? He's nice, he's fun, and Detective Sergeant Vizzini has never heard of him. Which counts for a lot when you live with my mother."

"You guys are so blind!" Griffin raved.

"I know what your problem is," said Pitch decisively. "You're jealous. You don't like him because we do. And you're afraid you're being replaced by a guy who's so helpful he's practically the other Man With The Plan!"

If she had plunged a knife into his back and twisted it, she could not have caused Griffin more pain.

C leopatra, the capuchin monkey, expertly climbed the ladder-back chair. With a spring of her agile little body, she launched herself over the dining room table, sailing just under the chandelier. As she passed, a little hand came up and clinked a dangling crystal. She landed delicately on the far end of the table and dropped to the floor.

Next, two black-tipped ears appeared on the launch chair. Blue eyes and whiskers rose up over the plane of the table. Penelope leaped, powered by muscular haunches. The Siamese followed the monkey's path, swiping and missing the chandelier with an immaculate white paw, but tweaking the crystal with the dark tip of her elegant tail. She landed in the seat of the opposite chair before jumping down beside Cleopatra. The capuchin chattered appreciatively, and the two friends lined up to do it again.

A large black eye watched the goings-on balefully. Luthor lay on the hall rug just outside the dining room, forlorn and alone. He couldn't quite put his paw on it, but something was just not right here. This was *his* house, and Cleopatra was *his* friend. Yet here he was, on the outside looking in.

A mechanical roar interrupted his dark thoughts, and he felt a rough bump from behind.

Mrs. Drysdale prodded her daughter's big dog with the vacuum cleaner. "Move it, you big galoot. Why are you always underfoot? Honestly, you take up half the house!"

Luthor scrambled up, shaking himself all over. From the dining room he saw the cat staring at him with those luminous eyes. The thing was smirking — he was sure of it. He watched resentfully as cat and monkey went through another round of jumps.

Well, this was *his* table, long before any fancy cat showed up. . . . With an earsplitting bark, he galloped down the hall. By the time he hit the dining room, he was at full speed, ears flattened, eyes near slits. A monumental leap brought him up to the top of the chair. And, using it as a springboard, he launched himself over the table. The whole house shook as he scored a direct hit on the chandelier, sending crystal droplets flying in all directions, shattering against the walls and floor.

The power of his bound took him across the table, past the chair, and clear into the china cabinet against the far wall. The glass doors disintegrated, and the contents of the breakfront spilled out all over him —

plates, cups, and stemware bounced off his body and hit the hardwood, breaking into pieces.

Luthor's canine brain wasn't equipped to perceive cause and effect, but he was pretty sure this had not been one of his better ideas.

"*Savannah!*" howled Mrs. Drysdale. "Come and put your dog outside!"

When Savannah arrived on the scene and took in the destruction, her voice was not kind and soothing. She was angry with Luthor. And she wasn't angry with Cleopatra or the cat, who'd been engaged in exactly the same jumping game.

What Savannah actually said when she tied him up in the backyard was, "Why can't you be more like Penelope?"

OPERATION PHOENIX

GOAL: To discover the TRUTH about Victor Phoenix

STEP 1: Find the subject's old·SCHOOL.

Griffin frowned at the paper. If he'd had his whole team, Step 1 would have taken about eight seconds. Melissa could have gotten on her computer and traced Victor back to the hospital he was born in. But that was what was different about Operation Phoenix. Griffin Bing was tackling this plan on his own.

Griffin had only one class with Victor where the others weren't around — science, in third period. They weren't lab partners, of course. Victor wanted nothing to do with him, and the feeling was definitely mutual.

But today, Griffin sidled up to the new kid. "Hey, Victor, what do you say we work on this experiment together?"

The blue eyes were ice-cold. "I say no."

"Aw, come on," Griffin blustered. "What are we supposed to do — heat up this pink stuff?" With a carefully aimed elbow, he knocked over the beaker. Viscous pink liquid covered the counter and oozed over the edge to cascade onto Victor's backpack. "Oh, sorry, man!" He grabbed a paper towel and ducked down under the counter.

"It's fine," Victor said through clenched teeth. "Just let me do my own work!"

"No, I got this!" The pack was unbuckled, so it was easy enough to check out the contents while scrubbing at the stain. Textbooks, binders, a phone, and a tuna fish sandwich wrapped in plastic. Wait — what was this? There was a vinyl pencil case with a logo sticker on it in the shape of a bird of prey. Griffin squinted at it.

BASS JUNCTION M.S. HAWKS

"Cut it out!" Suddenly, the backpack was yanked away, nearly taking half of Griffin's nose with it.

Griffin stood up. "I was only trying to help."

"I don't need your help. You've helped enough." He stormed across the room and set up at a different experiment counter.

Griffin let him go. Bass Junction — another Long Island town about twenty miles to the east. He had what he wanted, *and* the satisfaction that Victor now had pink slime on his pants.

The next morning, Ben showed up as usual on Griffin's doorstep. "Let's hurry," Ben urged. "I don't want to be late."

"What do you mean late?" Griffin told him. "There's plenty of time."

Ben shook his head. "Savannah's bringing Victor's cat in today."

Griffin stared at his friend. "And you care about this because . . . ?"

"Victor's been running lines with Logan for his next audition, so he hasn't been able to visit Penelope," Ben explained. "It's kind of a big reunion."

"I hope you brought a ball of yarn for the happy couple."

Ben bristled, causing Ferret Face to peer out a sleeve in indignation. "You know, Griffin, Victor's a really nice guy. You'd like him if you'd give him a chance."

"I gave him a chance," Griffin said tersely. "He's the one who didn't give *me* a chance. And anyway, I'm not going to be there to witness this tender moment. I've got a doctor's appointment."

"Didn't you just go in a few weeks ago?" Ben asked.

"I had chills last night. Better not get too close. Give my regards to the bride and groom."

"You're so mean," Ben complained. "You know, I haven't been this itch-free since I first got Ferret Face. Putting egg in his hamburger has changed my life. I'm sure Victor could help you, too, if only you'd talk to the guy. Maybe you wouldn't have to go to the doctor so often."

"Victor wouldn't give me the skin off a grape, and even if he did, I wouldn't take his advice. See you tomorrow." Griffin closed the door with more of a slam than he'd been planning.

He watched his friend head for school alone and regretted the shadow that was growing between them. Under normal circumstances, Griffin would have recruited Ben to join him on the mission he had planned for today. But Ben was on Team Victor now — every bit as much as the others, maybe even more. Who would have thought that saving him from a little bit of ferret fur could have bought his loyalty like this? It seemed to Griffin that long-term friendship should mean more.

Well, Ben was just going to have to learn the hard way.

It took three buses and more than an hour to get to Bass Junction, and then another half-hour walk to the middle school. Getting inside was the next order of business. Of course, Griffin totally looked the part of an eighth grader, but he had no idea how strict the security was in this place. He was about to enter the front door and approach the guard at the desk, when he noticed students pouring out of a side entrance into the school playground. He checked his watch. This must be the early lunch recess. Perfect. He didn't have to find his way in. They were coming out to meet him.

He waded into the crowd and approached a group of boys and girls sitting under a tree. "How's it going?" he greeted. "Do any of you guys remember a kid named Victor Phoenix? He used to go here."

Heads shook all around.

"We're sixth graders," one girl supplied. "We were in elementary last year."

Undaunted, Griffin forged on. One boy said the name sounded familiar, but he couldn't quite place it. Another acknowledged several Victors and a couple of Vics, but no Phoenix. A kid with flaming red hair told him a long boring story about his friend Hector Phoenix from summer camp. Hector lived in Maryland.

Griffin tried to be patient. "No, it's definitely not him. The kid I'm talking about is kind of small and skinny, with blond hair that he spikes with a lot of gel. And his name's not Hector; it's Victor. Victor Phoenix."

"Wait a minute," came a low, gravelly voice behind him. "You're not talking about Victor Feeney?"

Griffin turned to come face to chest with a football type, a beast of a boy who was at least Vader-sized.

"I'm pretty sure it's Phoenix," Griffin replied. "Small kid? Blond?"

The beast snorted. "So he calls himself Phoenix now. He wishes. Victor the Victim was a walking wedgie waiting to happen."

"And he happened in a lot of places," added Beast's sidekick, who was only slightly smaller. "All up and down this yard."

"He used to get picked on?" Griffin asked, to make sure he understood what he was hearing. The great Victor Phoenix who had waltzed into Cedarville to be immediately loved and admired by all?

"It was kind of the national pastime around here," Beast explained. "When that kid left town, all the other nerds moved up one space. Not that we'll ever come across another one like him."

"It's true," the sidekick added. "Sometimes I miss him. I've been pants-ing Seth Bornstein, but it's just not the same."

"And the name is definitely Feeney?"

"Rhymes with *weenie*," the sidekick confirmed wanly. "Nothing rhymes with *Bornstein*."

"You're *sure* it's Feeney?" Griffin persisted.

Beast's face darkened. "You spend enough time with your fist around the waistband of someone's underwear, you know his last name. You want me to find out *your* last name?"

Griffin backed away quickly. Getting hung by the tighty-whities on a fence post wasn't part of the plan. And there were plenty of words that rhymed with *Bing*. For the first time, he felt a twinge of appreciation for Darren Vader. At least Darren was a clown instead of just pure mean. There was zero humor in these two Neanderthals. But he was grateful to them in one way: He'd always known there was something not quite right about Victor Phoenix. And this trip had proven it.

He hung around for the rest of lunch, giving the Neanderthals a wide berth and talking to a few other people. The picture of Victor Phoenix — now Victor Feeney — began to fill out. Not everyone was as nasty as the Neanderthals, but Victor had definitely been bullied at Bass Junction. He was a small, slight kid, quiet and very smart. And while most students had no problem with him, once his reputation had been cemented as Victor the Victim, it had proved impossible to shake. In a way, Victor could have been the poster boy for the anti-bullying assembly at Cedarville.

No wonder the kid hates me, Griffin thought. *After Darren's little speech, he assumes I'm exactly the kind of jerk who made his life so miserable here.*

A few of the Bass Junction kids even wondered aloud whether the family's move had been to get their son out of this school.

"Who's asking about Victor Feeney?" came an adult voice. Fingers pointed and the teacher's eyes fixed on

Griffin. "What are you doing here? This is a closed campus. You're not one of our students."

"Sorry," Griffin said quickly. "I was just leaving, anyway." He began to edge his way out of the school yard.

"You know Victor?" the teacher persisted.

Griffin nodded. "He goes to my school now."

She hesitated for a moment, her expression a mixture of suspicion and regret. "Tell him we're all rooting for him. Tell him — that we're sorry. We should have fought harder for him, but we didn't know how."

"I will," Griffin said uncomfortably, and was gone.

He might have mentioned that Victor's life at his new school was just fine. It was fine because it was Griffin's life, stolen from Griffin, along with all Griffin's friends.

But after what Griffin had learned today, that was subject to change.

The meeting was called for seven p.m. that same day. Ben slipped gingerly through the gate into the Drysdales' yard, keeping a wary eye open for Savannah's big Doberman. If there was one thing Luthor inspired, it was respect. There was still a lot of guard dog left in the big guy, and Ben was convinced it was only a matter of time before it all came out. Today, however, Luthor's leash was tied around a fence post, limiting the big dog's range.

Ben was surprised. Savannah complied with Cedarville's leash laws, but at home, Luthor was given as much freedom as any other member of the family. If the Drysdales adopted a grizzly bear, it would be afforded the same rights. *And*, thought Ben, *it would probably be afraid of Luthor.*

Pitch, Logan, and Melissa were already there.

"Any clue what this is about?" Ben inquired.

Melissa shook her head, setting the curtain swinging.

"We were going to ask *you*. This whole thing is Griffin's idea."

"All I know is he had a doctor's appointment, and it must have run long, because he never made it to school."

"There was another news story about the missing lottery ticket on TV last night," Logan announced. "The final deadline ticking down — that whole angle. You don't think Griffin saw it and now he's gung ho to go after Darren again?"

"Not even Griffin is *that* nuts," Ben replied. "Hey, Savannah, how come Luthor's tied up?"

She stepped off the back deck and came to join them on the grass. "The poor sweetheart has some growing up to do. He hasn't reacted well to hosting Penelope. I would have thought he'd show more maturity about a houseguest."

"But he's used to having cats around," Pitch pointed out. "He's been living with Rosencrantz and Guildenstern for years."

Savannah's two American shorthairs were a pair of elderly gentlemen who treated the new Siamese like the royalty she considered herself to be. They followed a few steps behind her, loyal and faithful retainers, as she paced the lawn just outside the reach of Luthor's leash. She had to be doing it on purpose, just to drive Luthor crazy.

"If that rope breaks," Ben observed, "there won't be enough left of Penelope to fill a thimble."

Savannah glared at him. "Don't be ridiculous. He would never hurt her. He loves her. He's just acting out. Now, where's Griffin?"

As if on cue, Griffin rounded the corner of the house. "Great. You're all here. Listen up. I wasn't at the doctor's today. I went on a little fact-finding mission. I finally got the scoop on the mysterious Victor Phoenix."

Ben was outraged. "You *spied* on him?"

"Not on him — I took the bus to his old school in Bass Junction and talked to the people who used to deal with him every day. I *knew* there was something fishy about that guy. And sure enough, I was right."

"My stupid-detector is tingling," Pitch warned.

"For starters, he isn't Victor Phoenix — he's Victor *Feeney*. He couldn't even be honest about his own name. And you know why? Because the cool guy who rode into Cedarville on a white horse and swept you all off your feet is actually the biggest nerd that ever walked the earth!"

A babble of protest greeted this announcement.

Ben put everyone's feelings into words. "Really, Griffin? We're calling people nerds now? What are we? When I look in the mirror, I don't see Mr. Popularity. I see a runty kid with a ferret in his shirt. And the same goes for Melissa and her computers, Logan and his acting, Savannah and her animals, Pitch and her climbing, and you and your plans. We're not friends because we get invited to all the best parties and have to fight off the paparazzi together. We're friends because why shouldn't we be? And Victor's one of us now — regardless of what you found out in Bass Junction."

"You don't understand," Griffin persisted. "His nickname was Victor the Victim. He got picked on so much that it's one of the reasons his family moved. Don't you see? Vader made him think I'm a bully, so he hates me. And he's playing all of you to get you to hate me, too!"

Savannah stared at him. "So we shouldn't be friends with Victor because he got *bullied*?"

"Of course not!" Griffin struggled to express himself. "I feel terrible for the guy. You should have seen the knuckle draggers who were picking on him. They make Darren look like Prince Charming. But that doesn't mean I have to lay down my life so he can be happy — especially after he came here and lied to everybody, even about his last name."

"You know, Griffin," Pitch said coldly, "maybe Vader was right about you. You *are* a bully. What was Victor supposed to do — tattoo the word 'DWEEB' on his forehead? It's not like a severe allergy, where you have to wear a bracelet so everybody knows."

"It's horrible how he was treated at that school," Logan added. "Who can blame him for wanting to be a different person?"

"I told you I feel bad for him," Griffin acknowledged. "But that doesn't change the fact that he bamboozled —"

"Weren't you paying attention at the assembly?" Pitch challenged. "There's no excuse for pushing some poor kid around. So what if Victor's using a different last name? Does that mean he deserves to be treated like a punching bag? Same thing with Darren. What we did to him was wrong. He's not the nicest guy in the world, but that doesn't make it okay."

"We were with you with Darren," put in Ben. "And we all got in a lot of trouble for it. We're not going to make the same mistake with Victor."

At that moment, the sliding door opened and the subject himself stepped into the backyard. "Your mom said you were out here. Hi, guys." Victor's gaze skipped over Griffin and came to rest on Penelope. "There's my girl!"

The Siamese strolled over to sniff at him, then moved on to Savannah and meowed to be picked up.

Savannah gave him a sympathetic smile. "She's not ignoring you. It's just that I'm the one who's feeding her now."

When she took the cat into her arms, Luthor began to struggle at the end of his leash, whining and barking. "Oh, behave yourself," Savannah said crossly. "Act your age."

Luthor threw himself forward in one mighty lunge. The leash snapped him back, and he collapsed to the grass, half strangled, and whimpering.

Griffin gazed at him with undisguised sympathy. "I'm with you, big guy. You think you know people, and they forget you were ever their friend."

He spun on his heel and stormed out of the yard.

When Ben knocked on Griffin's door the next
morning on his way to school, he was surprised
when the door was answered by Mrs. Bing.

"Oh, you just missed him, Ben," she assured him.
"He left no more than two minutes ago."

It set off warning bells in Ben's head. Griffin
always waited for him, and they *always* walked to
school together — except on days like yesterday, when
one of them had a doctor's appointment, or the flu, pel-
lagra, or whatever. Only Griffin hadn't *really* been sick
yesterday. Ben had a sinking feeling that the reason
his friend had left without him this morning had a lot
to do with that — his trip to Victor's old school and
the confrontation with the team that had followed.

"I think we have some leftover bacon for Ferret
Face," Mrs. Bing offered.

"Oh, no, thanks. I'll catch up with Griffin." He ran off.

Ferret Face was displeased, as if he knew he'd just
missed out on something good. Or maybe he was

just nauseated. He occasionally suffered motion sickness brought on by Ben's uncoordinated gallop.

Ben spied his friend just stepping onto the school grounds and rushed over to enter with him. "You didn't wait for me."

Griffin kept his gaze straight ahead. "I didn't think you were coming."

"What are you talking about? I come every day. Since kindergarten!"

"I just assumed you'd be walking with Victor this morning."

Ben groaned. So here it was. The same determination and singleness of purpose that made Griffin The Man With The Plan also made him the most stubborn, mule-headed, inflexible, infuriating person alive. The team was just making sure Griffin couldn't dump all over Victor, but Griffin refused to see that.

Ben wished he could go back in time to glue Pitch's mouth shut before she called Victor "the new Man With The Plan." But it was too late. Now Griffin was going to make this into a war. And as his best friend, Ben was going to end up on the front lines.

"Griffin, don't be like that," he pleaded.

"I'm not being like anything," Griffin shot back. "I'm the same as I always was. It's you guys who are different. I can accept it from the others, but not you, Ben. And Savannah, too, after all the hoops I've jumped through for her wacko monkey and her vicious dog."

Ben made one last effort. "You're turning this into a

big deal for nothing. All that's happened is this: A new guy showed up. We like him. So what? It doesn't change anything about you."

"You're wrong. It changes everything."

It was classic Griffin. Once he dug in his heels about something, it took an M1 tank to move him.

Nor was Griffin content to vent his opinions only to his closest friend. The whole team was fair game.

In second period, Pitch approached Ben. "What's up with Griffin? Don't tell me he's going to make a federal case out of this Victor thing."

Or Logan: "What's the matter with Griffin? He just told me that I'll never make it in Hollywood because I don't know the meaning of loyalty, and none of the big directors will want to work with me!"

Savannah was more practical. "I couldn't be more grateful for the things Griffin has done for Cleo and Luthor and me. But that doesn't give him the right to tell me who I can be friends with."

Shy Melissa said nothing, but Ben could make out her anguished eyes behind her curtain of hair. She would never have had any friends if Griffin hadn't drafted her onto the team. To be caught between her allegiance to him and doing what was right must have been tearing her apart.

Even Darren could not help but notice the rift that was opening between Griffin and his friends. "Trouble in paradise," he crowed. "It's beautiful. I only hope I can take credit for at least some of this."

"You can." Ben was surprised at how angry his voice sounded. "You called him a bully in front of the whole school."

"I know." Darren chortled. "Man, I'm good."

Maybe that was the key to ending this standoff — to convince Victor that there was no bully in Griffin Bing. So Ben tried over lunch. But with every single team member clamoring for Victor's attention, the poor kid didn't have enough ears to go around. And it didn't help that Griffin himself sat alone on the other side of the cafeteria, glowering at them. It was hard to sell him as a good guy when he looked like that.

It reminded Ben of one of those movies where a simple misunderstanding just grows until it becomes so close to insurmountable that even the audience can't stand it. If Victor had showed up a couple of days sooner and gotten to know the real Griffin, none of this would be happening. It was bad timing, nothing more. And yet with each passing hour, the parties grew more resentful, and the problem became that much less fixable.

Ben took one more stab at Griffin on the way home from school. "Griffin, if Victor really thinks you're a bully, all you have to do is convince him that you're not. How hard can that be? I'll help."

The look Griffin shot him in reply confirmed Ben's worst fears. His friend had spent the day aggrieved and alone, stewing in his own resentment. He was miles beyond reason. "If he's wrong about me," he challenged darkly, "how come that's *my* problem?"

Ben played his trump card. "Surely, The Man With The Plan can see how easy it is to clear this up. It would be the simplest plan you ever made."

"You don't need *me* for planning," Griffin said sarcastically. "You've got the *new* Man With The Plan. If he's such a great planner, let *him* make everything right. And while he's at it, maybe he can think up a way to get Ferret Face elected president. Then Victor will have to train something else to bite you when you fall asleep, like a rattlesnake, or a black widow spider. There are still a few wrinkles to iron out, but I'm sure he's up to the challenge. The genius of planning is in the details."

It stung. Ben was only trying to help, for Griffin's sake more than anybody's.

"Those details you think you're so good at — Victor's good at them, too, mostly because he considers other people's opinions, not just his own. But your plans have to be one hundred percent Bing, don't they? Your way or no way. So have it your way! You always do!"

They walked home on opposite sides of the street.

O *ur next award is a new prize for us on the Nobel*
Committee. Our first-ever Nobel Prize in Planning
goes to a teenage gentleman from Cedarville, United
States. . . ."

Griffin stood up and shot Albert Einstein a know-
ing wink as one Nobel laureate to another.

"We salute Mr. Victor Phoenix!"

"No!" Griffin protested, shocked. "He's not The
Man With The Plan! I am! And his name isn't even
Phoenix!"

But the applause in the auditorium drowned out
his words.

"This is a mistake!" Griffin raved as a tri-
umphant Victor accepted his medal. "That's my
prize! He's no planner! All he does is buy people's
friendship!"

"Don't be a bully, young man," Dr. Einstein
scolded.

"I'm not a bully!" Griffin howled.

"I believe you are," the renowned genius returned. *"I know it as surely as E equals mc squared."*

"No! No! No . . . !"

The bedroom lights came on and Griffin awoke to find his father shaking him. "Everything's okay, kid. You're having a bad dream."

Griffin sat up in a cold sweat. "The worst." It was awful enough that Victor had hijacked Griffin's team. Now he'd even wormed his way into Griffin's favorite dream, and turned Einstein against him. It was enough to keep a guy from ever allowing himself to fall asleep again.

"Mom and I have noticed that Ben hasn't been coming around for the past few days. Come to think of it, the phone hasn't been ringing off the hook, either. We just figured the gang wasn't too thrilled about garbage detail. But I'm starting to think maybe that's not the whole picture."

Griffin started to say *No big deal* but stopped himself, because it *was* a big deal. It was a huge, horrible deal. Obviously, he'd had arguments and disagreements with his friends, even Ben, over the years. But never could he have imagined that the entire team — lock, stock, and barrel — would turn against him like this. And over what? A creepy little phony who was worming his way into their good graces with Oscar predictions and ferret remedies! And Pitch had the *nerve* to call him the new Man With The Plan! His only real plan was to steal Griffin's place among his friends so he wouldn't have to be Victor the Victim in Cedarville, too.

But he couldn't bear to explain all this to Dad. So he just mumbled, "Sorry to wake you up. It's nothing for you and Mom to worry about."

School was the worst, because at every turn, he was treated to the sight of one or more of his friends hanging out with Victor. He was constantly swapping cat stories with Savannah. Suddenly, Logan couldn't rehearse with anybody else. He had Melissa upgrading some thingamajig on his computer so he'd have instant videoconferencing with all his new friends — as if they didn't spend enough time together at school, joined at the hip. And Ben — that was the one that really hurt. Ben was telling everyone who would listen how he'd never seen Ferret Face take to anybody the way he had to Victor. Not even Savannah, and all animals adored her. The whole thing was nauseating.

The bitterest pill of all was eating alone in the cafeteria. Not only did he feel like an outcast, but it was on display for the whole world to see. Griffin couldn't imagine anything worse.

"Hey, Bing." An overladen tray thumped down to the table beside him. "How's it going?"

"Beat it, Vader."

"No can do," Darren said briskly. "Remember the anti-bullying assembly? It counts as a good deed to befriend some pathetic loser, exiled to Siberia, thrown aside like a piece of trash. I might put in for extra credit for this."

"I remember that assembly," Griffin said between clenched teeth. "That's the one where you called me a bully."

"I didn't call you anything," Darren noted, defending himself. "I just looked at you, and everybody drew their own conclusions. Anyway, it serves you right for sending me digging through the garbage."

"I didn't send you. Your greed sent you."

"Good one!" Darren laughed appreciatively, showering a fine spray of soup over Griffin's tray. "I don't deny it. I love money. It drives me crazy to know that ticket is still out there. Thirty million bucks. Woo-hoo!"

Griffin rolled his eyes. "You're kidding, right? You know that was a fake article. We cooked it up on Melissa's computer."

Darren shook his head. "That's not the point. The article may be fake, but the ticket is one hundred percent real."

"Yeah," Griffin retorted, "a year ago. For sure it's long gone, burned up in some fireplace, or flushed down a toilet. Or it could be in a landfill, bulldozed down thirty feet, with a miniature golf course built on top of it."

Darren looked pained. "Don't talk that way about thirty million dollars."

Griffin had to laugh. "Anyway, it'll all be over in ten days. On day eleven, it's not worth one cent."

Darren dropped his sandwich so he could cover his ears. "I'm not listening," he mumbled, mouth full.

Griffin picked up his tray, even though his lunch was only half finished. "If you don't want to face reality, that's fine with me. But I'm telling you Superman couldn't find that ticket."

"Maybe not *Super*man," Darren conceded, his piggy eyes open so wide that his gaze almost seemed sincere. "But what about . . . a man with a plan?"

Light dawned on Griffin. "You sleaze. You hate my guts, but you don't mind using me to help you find some money."

"I don't hate you," Darren protested innocently. "In fact, now that everybody else hates you, I'm starting to appreciate what you've got to offer."

"I don't have anything to offer *you*," Griffin said bitterly. And he bused his tray and left the cafeteria.

13

So what do you think?"

Griffin looked up from the table in amazement. It was the next day at lunch. Twenty-four hours had passed, and Darren was continuing their conversation practically in mid-sentence.

"What part of 'buzz off' didn't you understand?" Griffin said wearily.

True to form, Darren could not be rebuffed. "I've been working on a list of the things I'm going to get when I cash in that ticket. And you know what I found out? Thirty million is so much money that even I can't spend it all. I mean, after the first ten or fifteen mil, you run out of stuff to buy. It's a dilemma."

Griffin stood, picked up his tray, and headed for an open table. If he had to listen to another word of this, not only would he lose his appetite, but the portion of lunch he'd already eaten would threaten to back up on him.

Thump!

The collision rattled all the cutlery on his tray and overturned his carton of chocolate milk. He looked up to see Ben standing there, his heart in his eyes.

"Griffin," he whispered, "are you really so sore at everybody that you'd rather sit with *Darren* than come over and have lunch with us?"

"I can eat where I please," Griffin retorted.

"Sure, but why would you *want* to? You have *friends*!"

Griffin looked over at his regular lunch spot. There sat Pitch, Savannah, Logan, and Melissa beside Ben's empty chair. At the head of the table, in the seat usually reserved for Griffin, was Victor holding court. Griffin couldn't make out their conversation, but the others were hanging on Victor's every word.

"I don't have any friends over there." He turned his back on Ben and rejoined Darren.

"That ticket is findable," Darren went on, again as if no interruption had taken place. "A really smart guy once said you can do anything if you've got the right plan."

Griffin knew he was being buttered up, but it still felt good to hear it, even coming from Darren. He wasn't getting credit for much these days. "*Almost* anything," Griffin amended magnanimously. "After all, no plan can help you eat lava, or turn coleslaw into gold bars."

"So you're with me?" Darren looked pleased.

"Forget it, Vader. That ticket is long gone."

"Correction. That ticket *might* be long gone. Which also means it might be lying around somewhere, ripe for the plucking."

It might, thought Griffin with a sigh. *Just like I might someday be friends with this jerk.*

But neither possibility seemed very likely.

"It's a beautiful day outside," Mrs. Bing announced to her son.

Griffin was flopped on the couch, eyes riveted on the TV, not even glancing away to reach into the chip bowl and feed his face. "I'm busy."

The theme music from *SpongeBob SquarePants* filled the den.

"No son of mine is going to waste a glorious Saturday watching cartoons you've already seen fifty times," she persisted. "Call Ben."

"There is no Ben," he told her.

She looked worried. "You two have been friends forever. Whatever's gone wrong between you, I'm sure it can be worked out."

"Well, as long as *you're* sure," he mumbled sarcastically.

"Griffin, I'm not the enemy here. I'm trying to help you. But if you insist on making yourself miserable, do it outside, where you can get some exercise and fresh air."

Griffin ended up meandering around on his bike, because it was easier than arguing. To Mom, even a full-scale zombie invasion wasn't too bad so long as you weren't stuck indoors on a beautiful day.

He already knew he wouldn't enjoy the ride, because everything in Cedarville reminded him of his friends. There was Ben's street and, a little farther along, the Dukakis house, where Melissa had done some of her greatest electronics work. As he passed Park Avenue Extension, he could see the old house in front of the water tower — scene of the plan that had brought the team together for the very first time. And down the way a little was where they'd put Luthor through the truck wash because it was the only way to give him a bath. Everywhere Griffin pedaled conjured up happy memories calculated to make him sad.

As he rode along the bike path in the park, lost in his melancholy, a loud buzzing swelled in his ears, and a sharp wind ruffled his hair. Alarmed, he risked a glance over his shoulder in time to see a large model airplane roar past, its wingtips missing his face by no more than six inches.

He watched in shock as the craft banked and came back around for another run at him. He ducked as it flew over, causing him to lose control of his bike. He swerved off the path. His tires bit into soft earth, and he wiped out on the grass. He disentangled himself from the frame and gawked as the remote control plane coasted in for a perfect landing on the lawn.

Standing there applauding and cheering this fancy flying were the same people who used to applaud and cheer for Griffin — Savannah, Logan, Pitch, Melissa, and Ben. And at the center of the group, operating the controls, was Victor Phoenix.

14

G riffin had read in books about a red haze of fury coming over someone's vision. But until this moment, he'd never experienced it. He could actually see the scene on the lawn through a fiery glow — Victor wielding the remote like a conquering hero, adored by all except Savannah, who was playing lovingly with Penelope. Luthor watched this, and the big dog looked none too pleased about it.

As Griffin ditched the bike and closed the distance between himself and his former friends, Penelope began to stalk the plane as if she were a great jungle cat after prey. Playfully, Victor began to reverse the craft away from her, jerking it back from each pounce. The others laughed as if it were the cleverest thing they'd ever seen — why not use an airplane as a cat toy after you've already used it to dive-bomb an innocent cyclist? How cute.

Luthor must have thought so, too. If it could be a cat toy, he reasoned, why not a dog toy? He jumped at it with a gentle swipe of his large paw. Victor quickly moved the plane to safety, and Savannah got in her Doberman's face. "No!" she admonished firmly. "You're too big to do what Penelope does! Act your age!"

Had Griffin not been totally focused on Victor, he might have noticed that Luthor did not back down, his ears flattening in defiance.

Ferret Face was the first to spot Griffin, followed rapidly by his owner.

"Griffin — you came!" Ben's hopeful expression faded as he noticed the hot anger radiating from his friend.

Griffin rounded on Victor. "Hey, Feeney, what's the big idea of buzzing me with that plane? How'd you like the next flight to be straight up your nose?"

Victor blanched, and Griffin backed off, thinking of the two Neanderthals from Bass Junction. *He probably thinks I'm serious!*

The others also noticed Victor's reaction.

"Chill out, Griffin!" said Pitch.

But Griffin was not to be silenced. "I'm sick of this phony playing the bully card! What do you call what he just did to me with that plane? I half killed myself falling off my bike!"

"I didn't do it on purpose," Victor replied, tight-lipped. "I couldn't."

"Really?" Griffin challenged. "Because going by your fan club here, you could fly that thing through the eye of a needle, so don't tell me it was an accident! I'm not as gullible as these guys."

"Come on, Griffin," Ben pleaded. "Hang out a little bit. The plane is really cool."

"I got a closer view of the plane than any of you! If I hadn't hit the dirt, it would be embedded in my skull. It better not happen again!"

He stormed away. There were a few halfhearted calls for his return, but not many, and not for long. So much for loyalty.

As he made his way back to his bike, he heard the plane taking off again.

If he's coming after me for round two . . .

He looked over his shoulder just as the craft left the ground. As it passed over the group, Luthor made one last attempt to prove that he could play with this new toy better than any cat. Poised on his muscular haunches, he sprang straight up, clamping his strong jaws around the fuselage and wrestling the craft back to the ground. He seemed pretty proud of himself as he set the crushed model down at Savannah's feet, the propeller still sputtering.

It was the one thing that could have brightened Griffin's mood. "Nice catch, buddy!" he called, and continued on, laughing.

Not even the sounds of the busy park could cover Savannah's scolding. *"Luthor-how-could-you-look-at-the-damage-you've-done-you-broke-Victor's-plane-it's-in-pieces-what-were-you-thinking-I-don't-know-what's-come-over-you!"*

Griffin would never have believed that anything

could come between Savannah and her beloved sweetie. His brow clouded. Of course, he never would have believed anything could come between himself and Ben, either, and there it was.

Back on his bike, Griffin was heading for the park entrance when he suddenly noticed he had company. Luthor was loping along beside him like he always loped along beside Savannah's bike.

Luthor normally terrified Griffin — and pretty much everybody else in Cedarville. But seeing the Doberman's destructive power unleashed on Victor's plane made the big guy a friend instead of a threat. "Too bad there's no dog Olympics. That performance would have been pure gold."

Luthor continued to follow the bike, even as Griffin started onto the path to exit the park.

Griffin stopped and dismounted. Luthor sat waiting.

"You'd better go back now. Savannah's calling."

The Doberman stared straight ahead and didn't budge.

"Hey, don't worry about the cat. In the end, you're the real sweetie."

Luthor was still as a statue.

With a sigh, Griffin got back on his bike and pedaled over toward where Victor and the group were standing. Melissa was trying to repair the broken plane and assuring Victor that it could be done. The damage was only structural; the engine and propeller shaft were intact.

Savannah stepped forward. "Thanks for bringing him back," she told Griffin, and turned to her dog. "Luthor, I was worried when I couldn't find you. Why did you run off?"

Luthor wouldn't even look at her.

"All right, sweetie. I know what this is about. You're jealous of Penelope. But why? You're not jealous of Cleo, or Rosencrantz and Guildenstern, or Arthur, or Lorenzo, or any of the others. You have to accept Penelope the same way."

Savannah hoped her soothing and reasonable tone and sincere expression would communicate what she was trying to tell him. It was this ability that made her Cedarville's number one dog whisperer. Yet now, even her most earnest dog whispering rolled off the Doberman's raised hackles. He was just too angry, too hurt.

"I never thought I'd say this," Griffin began, "but I'm with Luthor. Maybe you don't know as much about animals as you think you do, because he's right and you're wrong."

To his surprise, Savannah nodded sadly. "I agree with you. I'm not the animal expert I thought I was. Luthor is spoiled. It's not his fault; it's mine. I gave him my heart without considering the effect it might have on him. That's why he's being so willful and stubborn. And the only way to undo the damage I've done is by showing him some tough love."

Griffin bristled. Was that what they were doing to

him, too? "I'm out of here," he said disgustedly. He picked up the fallen leash. "Let's go, Luthor. You're coming with me."

Ben stared at him in disbelief. "You're not serious!"

But Savannah was pathetically grateful. "Really, Griffin? You'd take him? It would only be temporary — to give the tough love a chance to work. Of course we'll be together again. Luthor and I are soul mates."

"I'm not taking him for tough love," Griffin retorted. "I'm taking him because he needs to get away from that cat."

"He'll eat your house!" Ben blurted.

"I'll never forget this," Savannah went on emotionally. "If I didn't know it was for Luthor's own good, I'd be crying my eyes out at the thought of parting with him — and that he wants to leave me." To belie this courage, two big tears squeezed from her eyes and rolled down her pale cheeks. "He likes a cotton blanket — polyester is too itchy, and wool makes him sneeze."

Griffin turned to Victor. "Nice work. You happy now?"

Victor was speechless, and looked highly distressed, although that might have been about his crushed plane.

Griffin mounted his bike. "Come on, Luthor. Let's go home."

Luthor followed without a backward glance.

The SweetPick was back.

The photography had been completed, the new patent application signed, sealed, and delivered. Mr. Bing was tinkering with the device on his workbench with the garage door open when Griffin rode up, Luthor galloping alongside.

"Darnedest thing!" the inventor exclaimed. "I picked up the prototype from Daria Vader and there's a dent in the Safe-chete blade. Must have happened at the photographer's."

Face burning, Griffin dismounted and picked up Luthor's leash. What he needed was to change the subject.

Luckily, he had the perfect topic all cued up. "Dad, I've got Luthor with me."

"Whoa! So you do." Mr. Bing rushed out of the garage, hastily closing the door behind him. The Doberman had trashed his workshop in the past, and it had taken weeks to set everything right again. The adults of

Cedarville weren't much less intimidated by Savannah's big dog than their kids were. "What's that about? Where's Savannah?"

Griffin took a deep breath. "Well, I was wondering if he could come live with us."

Mr. Bing stared at his son and then burst out laughing. "Good one, Griffin. No, seriously."

"I *am* serious. It's kind of a long story, but he can't stay at the Drysdales'. It'll only be for a little while."

The conversation soon expanded to include Mrs. Bing. "But, Griffin," she reasoned, "we're not a pet family. We've never even had goldfish."

At any other time, Griffin would have agreed with her. But now when he looked at Luthor rejected and cast out, thanks to Victor's cat, he saw himself rejected and cast out, thanks to Victor.

"He's got nowhere else to go," he said simply.

In the end, one factor tipped the scales in Luthor's favor. Griffin was having problems with his friends. Perhaps a dog would provide the companionship he was missing.

"A dog, maybe, but that's not a dog; that's a moose!" hissed Mr. Bing.

"Don't be silly," his wife told him. "Luthor's well trained. He's competed in dog shows."

Savannah stopped by at dinnertime, struggling under an enormous bag of dog food that was nearly as tall as she was. Her eyes, red-rimmed from crying, looked haunted. It had only been a few hours since the incident in the park. But it was obvious that her program of tough love was tougher on her than it was on Luthor.

She kept peering past Griffin in the doorway, hoping to catch a glimpse of her beloved Doberman. "Where is he?"

"He's in the den, watching TV with my dad." Griffin couldn't resist adding, "Like it's any of your business after you drove him away."

"He loves *Lassie* and any of the *Balto* movies," she advised. "But no *Marley and Me*. It depresses him."

"If you don't want him depressed," Griffin said stonily, "ditch the cat."

Despite her heartbreak, Savannah was adamant. "I couldn't do that to Penelope, and it would be wrong for Luthor, too. I'd be telling him that he can get what he wants through bad behavior. Think of the message that would send."

"Luthor doesn't get messages," he reminded her. "He's a dog."

"Animals may not read and write and speak our language, but they have a social and emotional intelligence far greater than humans." She handed over two dog dishes and a hard rubber bone riddled with large bite marks. "Here's his toothbrush. Don't forget to add a drop of lemon to his water. It helps calm his stomach. And he shouldn't sleep in a drafty place. . . ."

She had several more instructions, but she started sobbing, and Griffin couldn't make out what she was saying. Had he not been so angry with his friends, he would have been overcome with sympathy.

"Yeah, well, you know where to find him when you come to your senses about the cat." He was tempted to add: *And you know where to find* me *when you come to your senses about Victor.* But he held his tongue. He wouldn't give her — or *any* of them — the satisfaction.

Luthor turned out to be a surprisingly good house-guest. Although bedding was set out for him in the basement, he chose to bunk with Griffin. There was no one to tell him he couldn't. Aside from some snoring and the occasional thrashing nightmare, he was a quiet roommate. At least, Griffin was delighted to wake up alive after that first night.

Even Mom and Dad were beginning to appreciate the advantages of having a dog around. Luthor doubled as a living, breathing garbage disposal unit. There was virtually nothing the Doberman wouldn't eat. His appetite was as broad as it was never-ending. And Dad had already filed for a reduction in his home insurance rates because there was now a watchdog on the premises.

"I pity the poor burglar who tries to make a move on the SweetPick now," he chortled.

The main disadvantage of hosting Luthor was Savannah herself. She called ten times a day with "useful" tips on the care and feeding of an oversized Doberman. After the first few hours, Griffin stopped answering the phone whenever her number appeared on the caller ID. If she wanted to speak to him badly enough, she'd come over in person.

That's who Griffin was expecting when the bell rang rather insistently after dinner on Sunday — Savannah, with another squeeze toy, or doggie treat, or coat-thickening shampoo with flea repellent.

He flung the door wide and announced, "Would you please —"

There stood Darren Vader with his usual ingratiating smile. "Anyway," he greeted Griffin, "we should definitely start working on our plan."

"We have no plan," Griffin told him. "And stop acting like we're in the middle of a conversation."

Darren used his superior bulk to bull his way through the door. "Thanks for inviting me in. Now, the problem as I see it —" He found himself face to fang with Luthor, who was wearing his most unfriendly expression. "What's *he* doing here?"

Griffin grinned. "Luthor's with me now. He keeps away undesirables, so you better go home."

Darren snorted a laugh. "You're a great kidder. So check this out." From his pocket, he produced a ratty piece of paper and unfolded it.

OPERATION JACKPOT

GOAL: To GET #####

That was all there was.

"A little short on specifics," Griffin commented.

"I figured that's your department," Darren explained. "You being The Man With The Plan and all that. So basically, it's like this: We go to the convenience store in Green Hollow where the winning ticket was sold. We ask to see the owner, engage him in conversation —"

"And of course he remembers every lottery ticket he's ever sold from a year before," Griffin finished sarcastically. "Never mind that the winner might have been bought by a guy who was passing through town on his way to Alaska."

Darren shrugged. "It's possible, but the odds favor somebody local who plays Giga-Millions every week."

"Yeah, but a store like that has hundreds of customers. Ben's dad gets coffee there every day on his way to work —"

Griffin fell silent. He would have loved to kick Darren out, but something about this line of reasoning rang a bell inside his planner's brain. According to Ben, the owner knew Mr. Slovak so well that he always had his coffee waiting for him, just the way he liked it.

If he remembers coffee habits, chances are he remembers lottery habits, too.

"I recognize that face!" exclaimed Darren, pleased. "It's your Man-With-The-Plan face!"

"No, it isn't!" Griffin snapped. But he had to admit it. The idea intrigued him, and his mind was churning furiously. Yes, the ticket was probably destroyed or lost far beyond recovery. But nobody could be 100 percent sure of that. And focusing the search on the store that had sold the winning ticket was almost planlike — which was astounding coming from Darren, who was normally as creative as a pile of rocks. Even the name — Operation Jackpot — had a nice ring to it.

All at once, he was aware of a yearning the likes of which he'd never known before. It wasn't for the money, exactly, and not even for the pride and bragging rights of tracking down something that no one else had been able to for almost a year. No, what Griffin craved was the pure glory of a *plan*.

Victor had taken his team away, his friends away, his whole life away. But *this* the newcomer couldn't get his greasy hands on. Operation Jackpot may have started with the likes of Darren. But it was going to prove that Griffin Bing was the one true Man With The Plan.

"We'll split the money eighty-twenty." Darren took in Griffin's disgusted look and renegotiated. "All right, seventy-thirty. I deserve the bigger share, because the whole thing was my idea."

"It's not going to work that way, Vader."

"Don't be greedy," Darren admonished. "Thirty percent of thirty mil is still nine million bucks —"

Sensing Griffin bristling at the notion of being called greedy by the greediest kid in Cedarville, Luthor silenced Darren with a sharp bark.

"What I'm saying," Griffin explained patiently, "is that even if we find the ticket — which is a long shot — it still won't be ours. It will belong to the person who bought it and forgot about it a year ago."

"No fair!" Darren exploded. "You snooze, you lose! If it wasn't for us, the ticket would expire and he'd get nothing!"

"I agree. And whoever it is will probably want to give us a reward. It might even be a big reward. But that's up to the winner. No matter what he gives us — even if it's nothing — we're not tricking him, or cheating him, and we definitely won't be robbing him!"

Although money wasn't Griffin's main goal, he secretly couldn't deny how much the prospect of that reward appealed to him. He knew from Dad just how risky a career as an inventor could be. A fat check from a happy and appreciative Giga-Millionaire would be a much-needed safety net for the Bing family in case the SweetPick turned out to be a bust. If the guy was grateful enough, it could cover college and more. Thirty million dollars was an enormous windfall.

"Fine," Darren grumbled. "We'll work out the details when we've got the cash." He beamed. "Looks like we're partners, buddy."

Griffin glared at him. "We may be partners, but we're definitely not friends."

OPERATION JACKPOT — FIELD STRATEGY

Step 1 - Visit Mike's Woodstock Market, the STORE that sold the TICKET.

Step 2 - Talk to OWNER about regular LOTTERY CUSTOMERS.

Step 3 - Interview SUSPECTS.

PRIME CANDIDATES:

> People who are FORGETFUL/suffer possible MEMORY LOSS

> Disorganized/MESSY people

> People with POOR EYESIGHT who might MISREAD ticket numbers

> Hoarders

> People with SECOND HOMES and/or storage LOCKERS

> People who MOVED about one year ago

Mike's Woodstock Market was a twenty-minute bike ride from Cedarville. It was a tiny convenience store across the street from the Green Hollow train station. A sign in the window declared: PEACE AND LOVE AND PREPAID PHONE CARDS. The inside was cluttered with racks of snacks, groceries, newspapers, and magazines. Large refrigerators along the walls held dairy products and soft drinks. A self-serve doughnut and muffin bar stood at the rear.

Darren elbowed Griffin hard enough to fracture his ribs. He pointed at a sticker on the cash register: GIGA-MILLIONS LOTTERY: AUTHORIZED DEALER.

"We know that already," Griffin said impatiently. "That's why we're here."

He regarded the clerk behind the counter, an impossibly tall, impossibly thin man in his sixties, with long gray hair and a matching untrimmed beard.

"Mike?" Griffin ventured.

"Guilty," Mike acknowledged, with a wide smile that was missing at least two teeth. "What can I do for you, man?"

Griffin had trouble taking his eyes off the clerk's headband, which read FLOWER POWER in tiny beads. An ancient frilled poncho that might once have been a color completed the outfit.

Darren could not restrain himself. "Are you a hippie?"

"No, man." Mike sighed. "The whole hippie thing went totally commercial. I'm just a guy struggling to be true to himself. What a long, strange trip it's been. We're running a two-for-one special on Cheez Doodles, if you're interested."

"No, thanks," said Griffin. "I understand this was the store where that missing Giga-Millions ticket was sold."

Mike made a face. "Money. I don't see what all the fuss is about."

Darren indicated an instant-coffee jar bearing a hand-lettered sign: GIVE TO THE CREATION OF A WOODSTOCK MUSIC FESTIVAL NATIONAL HISTORIC SITE. "Seems like money's not so terrible when it suits you," he observed.

"Woodstock." The tall, thin man's face took on a far-off dreamy expression. "Greatest three days of my life. I only hope the human race can get back to that place before it chokes on its own greenhouse gases and reality TV!"

"And a historic site will do that?" asked Darren, taken aback by the intensity of the storekeeper's emotion.

"Well, it's a first step."

"Anyway," Griffin forged on, determined to keep the plan on track, "you've probably heard that the Giga-Millions ticket is going to expire on October sixth. So my friend and I had a crazy thought: What if the person who bought that ticket just forgot about it and stuffed it in a pocket or a junk drawer?"

Mike had lost interest in the conversation and was dusting off a display of glow-in-the-dark yo-yos.

"So," Griffin continued, "we were wondering if you would help us narrow down which one of your customers might have it."

Mike hung his shaggy head. "In the end, it always comes down to the almighty dollar."

"We don't want it for ourselves," Griffin put in quickly.

"That's okay. Nobody's going to use it to help the poor or feed the hungry, so you young dudes might as well have it. But it's not going to make you happy."

"I'm willing to suffer," Darren promised.

"Can you tell us about your regular lottery customers?" Griffin requested. "People who play Giga-Millions every week? Chances are it's one of them."

"I'm not so good with names, man. I'm not into labeling."

Griffin became aware of the first stirrings of that uneasy feeling he always got when a plan began to bog down. It was a really bad sign when it happened before the operation even got off the ground.

And then he was staring right at it. Over Mike's poncho-clad shoulder, a built-in videocam surveyed all the action that took place at the cash counter.

"You have a security camera!" Griffin exclaimed.

Mike nodded sadly. "Big Brother is keeping an eye on all of us."

"That's great!" Griffin exclaimed. "If your security company keeps video archives from a year ago, we can go back to last October sixth and see everybody who bought a Giga-Millions ticket here that day!"

The storekeeper made a face. "Back in the sixties, I joined protest marches against that kind of thing."

"But you'll do it, right?" Darren asked breathlessly.

Mike's response was a world-weary shrug of poncho fabric. "Anything for my fellow man, man."

It took some doing to get in touch with the store's security company and have them dig up the video footage from last October 6. It was all accomplished over the Internet, but Mike didn't know how to use his computer beyond the bar code scanner and the power switch. Not only did he look like a leftover from 1969, but his understanding of technology came from that year as well.

Eventually, Griffin managed to get the footage on the screen. Even fast-forwarding, it was going to take a long time to browse through an entire business day.

"Too bad we don't have Melissa," Griffin murmured.

"What for?" Darren yawned absently.

"You're kidding, right? She's a total computer genius. It would take her about three seconds to program a way to skip through all the hours where nothing's happening."

"If she could see the screen through all that hair."

"She's got more smarts in one strand of that hair

than you'll ever have in your entire body!" Griffin may have been angry at his friends, but that didn't mean he was going to let Darren put them down.

By trial and error, Griffin sped up the playback, and they made some real progress. Through a rounded wide-angle lens behind the counter, he and Darren watched an endless parade of faces make their purchases and move off. Whenever the Giga-Millions machine coughed out another ticket, they would call Mike over for a customer ID.

That was where the first stumbling block appeared. Mike knew everybody, but not exactly by name:

"That's the guy who's always whistling show tunes."

"She takes her muffins lightly toasted, no butter."

"I think his name is Dave — or maybe it's Percival."

"Oh, yeah, I remember that hat. He doesn't wear it anymore."

"I don't know her, but her brother drives that big BMW."

"Nobody goes through more sunflower seeds than that guy."

Griffin dutifully noted every comment, including the one about Mr. Slovak: "That dude keeps asking me to stock ferret food. What does he think this is — a pet shop?"

It turned out that October 6 had been a slow day for Giga-Millions at Mike's Woodstock Market. In all, the store had sold ninety-six tickets to forty-seven different buyers. Once the master list was finished, Griffin began to quiz Mike about who might fit the profile he'd created in the plan for Operation Jackpot: Was anybody forgetful or disorganized? Was poor eyesight a factor in the group? A reputation as a hoarder? Which customers had a second home, an apartment in the city, or a storage locker? Had one of the forty-seven moved around that time?

Mike had a lot of details, none of them worth very much. He recognized clothes. He could separate the Giants fans from the Jets fans. He knew what kind of wallets and pocketbooks his regulars had. He could connect faces with odors — Old Spice, sweat socks, bad breath, pickles, talcum powder, Axe body spray, chicken curry vindaloo.

That night, as Luthor wolfed down a mountain of dog food, The Man With The Plan sliced and diced his data in an attempt to work out the next step. This was the point where Melissa would know a computer program that would deliver the very piece of information he needed. Or, failing that, Pitch would make a sarcastic comment, or Ben would start complaining, and somehow, magically, Griffin would see exactly what he had to do. He'd never appreciated just how crucial his team really was. Now he realized how much he relied on them to function as a sounding board to focus his own thinking. Luthor's slavering and smacking of canine lips was a poor substitute.

First, he rearranged his list into logical categories:

FORGETFUL:

ALEX... surname UNKNOWN... Retired BOXER... memory
loss from too many punches?... Jeep Wrangler, wide
tires... address UNKNOWN...

POOR EYESIGHT:

Mrs. CLAUS (not real name... resembles SANTA's
wife)... thick GLASSES, horn-rimmed... address: SENIOR
CITIZENS' residence close to train station...

HOARDER:

Name: UNKNOWN... buys arts and crafts magazines...
wears homemade HATS with BEADS bought in store...
drives GREEN VAN packed with junk... address
UNKNOWN...

MOVED @ LAST OCTOBER

Name: JERRY (possibly HARRY)... surname UNKNOWN...
black leather JACKET, message: "HAWG WILD" in nail
studs... drives big HARLEY... address: UNKNOWN...

It went on and on. Forty-seven suspects, hundreds
of random details, most of them worthless. Not a single real address.

"How will I ever get through it all?" Griffin moaned
aloud.

Luthor interrupted his eating to cast him a sympathetic look, punctuated by a rolling burp.

One piece of data trumped all the others. It was the first of October. Only five days remained before the October 6 deadline. Then all this work would be worth exactly as much as the missing ticket.

Zero.

W here do you think you're going?"
His hand barely an inch from the front door-
knob, Griffin froze. His mother stood at the entrance
to the kitchen, arms akimbo.

"Out," he told her. "On my bike."

He figured that would satisfy her. Outside. Fresh
air. Exercise.

Alas, not so.

"Aren't you forgetting something?" she demanded.

"I'll wear a helmet."

"I'm not your pet sitter," she informed him. "You
can't just go gallivanting around town for hours, leaving me stuck with Luthor."

"I thought you liked him now, Mom."

"That's beside the point," she insisted. "He's not
my dog."

"He's not *my* dog, either. He's Savannah's."

She wouldn't budge. "You took him in. He's your
responsibility."

So Griffin started out on his bike with Luthor loping alongside at the end of his leash.

Darren was waiting at the meeting point. "Jeez, Bing, why'd you bring the mutt? People will slam the door in our faces when they see that monster."

Griffin didn't want Luthor on this mission any more than Darren did. But just hearing the challenge coming from his archenemy offended him on the Doberman's behalf. "That shows how much you know, Vader. Anyone can see what a sensitive and intelligent dog he is." He felt a twinge as he realized he sounded exactly like Savannah.

The leash was torn out of his hand the first time Luthor saw a butterfly to chase. But except for the occasional side trip to sniff interesting flora, fauna, or fire hydrant, the Doberman was content to gallop at more or less the same pace as the two bicycles.

When they made it to Green Hollow, their first stop was the Vandermere Senior Citizens' Residence, not far from the train station and Mike's Woodstock Market. Griffin was worried that dogs might not be allowed inside, but the security guard actually reached down and patted Luthor as they entered the sliding doors.

"The residents love pets," he commented.

Griffin couldn't help wondering if that statement would hold true if something spooked Luthor and he leveled the place.

The Man With The Plan approached the front desk.

"We're looking for an older lady. White hair pulled back in a bun, thick glasses, eyesight not so good . . ." With a sinking heart, he panned the lobby. There were at least fifteen women on the couches who matched that exact description.

"She looks like Santa's wife," added Darren. "You know, *ho, ho, ho*?"

The receptionist was annoyed. "There are more than three hundred residents here —" She caught sight of Griffin's printout from the store's security camera. "Oh, you want Sadie Weintraub. She's in 314. Take the elevator on your left."

Luthor loved the elevator, and it took both boys to drag him, whining and complaining, into the hall.

Mrs. Sadie Weintraub, aka Mrs. Claus, didn't get many visitors to her small, neat apartment, and was thrilled to see them.

If there had been any doubt about her eyesight, it was dispelled when she exclaimed, "Oh, what a lovely little puppy!"

Griffin and Darren exchanged a knowing glance. Mrs. Weintraub was a definite candidate. Anyone who could look at Luthor and see a puppy was more than capable of misreading the numbers on a lottery ticket.

Griffin cleared his throat. "I understand that you play Giga-Millions."

Mrs. Weintraub brightened. "Every week like clockwork. I buy my tickets from Mike down the street. Such a handsome young man."

Further evidence of failing vision: that she perceived Mike as (a) handsome and (b) young.

"Here's the thing." Griffin forged on as the old lady seated them at a small table and placed a burgeoning plate of homemade cookies between them. "There's a winning ticket missing, and it was sold at Mike's store. We're — uh — helping Mike make sure none of his favorite customers lose out on a big prize."

"That's very nice of you sweet boys," she said, setting two tall glasses in front of them. "Regular milk, or chocolate?"

"I'll take chocolate," mumbled Darren, his mouth full of cookie.

She rambled on about the weather, her late husband, Bernie, and a Yankee game she'd attended in 1961, in which both Roger Maris and Mickey Mantle had hit home runs.

Griffin struggled to keep the visit on topic. "So do you think you could be the one who misplaced that ticket?"

"That's impossible, dear," she explained. "I've been playing the same numbers for more than thirty years — my birthday, Bernie's birthday, nineteen, and forty-eight, for the year Harry Truman got elected. I read about that missing ticket. Those aren't the right numbers."

Griffin felt his hopes deflating like a balloon. As a planner, he understood that it was rare for an operation to succeed on the very first try. Yet he'd had a good feeling about Mrs. Claus, who fit the profile to a T. But here she was, with today's newspapers and the latest bestsellers on the coffee table, and the whole place tidy and sparkling clean. This woman was far too sharp to overlook a three-cent discrepancy on her grocery bill, much less a thirty-million-dollar lottery ticket.

They thanked her for the cookies and excused themselves, taking the stairs this time so Luthor couldn't fall in love with the elevator again.

As they left the building, Griffin caught sight of a middle-aged man stepping out of Mike's Woodstock Market.

Darren snickered. "Nice hat, doofus."

The man wore a crocheted cap covered in multicolored beads, and a handwoven vest over his shirt. He climbed into a green van and started away from the curb.

Griffin stared. Macramé window hangings covered everything but the windshield.

Beaded hat . . . green van packed with junk . . .

The hoarder!

M ister, come back!" Griffin called out.

But it was too late. The vehicle was already halfway down the street.

The two boys jumped on their bikes and took off after it, Luthor joining the chase and soon outstripping the cyclists. They lost sight of the van a few times, but the Doberman kept them on the trail. The driver turned onto a side street and slowed down, approaching his destination. The three pursuers fell into line behind the van and pulled up when it turned into the driveway of a small cottage.

The front porch confirmed that they'd indeed found their hoarder. It was clogged with lawn furniture and all manner of outdoor ornaments, from scowling gargoyles to colorful unicorns and patriotic eagles. Pots of varying sizes stood on every open surface, along with garden gnomes and unused walkway lights.

The man got out of the van and began to pick his way through the obstacle course to the front door.

Griffin jumped off his bike and nearly wiped out on a pink flamingo camouflaged by tall uncut grass. "Mister, can we talk to you?"

The man's eyes found Griffin, then Darren, and finally Luthor. "Keep your dog off my lawn."

"Sure thing." Griffin clipped the leash around the handlebars of his bike, and he and Darren approached the porch. "Mike sent us — you know, from the convenience store?" He outlined their quest for the missing ticket and their theory that one of the regular lottery customers might have misplaced it.

"It couldn't have been me," the man told him. "I check the numbers every week."

"Maybe you got too busy and forgot one time," Darren suggested.

The man shook his head. "I'm extremely organized."

Griffin and Darren took in the wreckage of the porch and the state of the property, which was overgrown and strewn with lawn accessories of all varieties, including two upended plaster lions and a concrete birdbath.

"Just in case, would you mind if we came inside and had a look around?" Griffin requested. "It would be a shame to throw away all that money just because of a little oversight."

"More than a shame. A personal tragedy . . . for me," Darren put in honestly.

The man adjusted the beaded cap and frowned. "I can't have the dog."

"Right," Griffin confirmed. "Just us."

Leaving Luthor clipped to the bike, they approached the small house and followed their host inside. Luthor rumbled a low complaint. He was used to the Drysdale rules, which stated that animals were entitled to all freedoms and privileges accorded to humans.

The interior made the chaos of the porch seem neat. Griffin had never been to the rain forest, but he'd always imagined it looking like this. Long macramé planters and hangings dangled so low from the ceiling, and random stuff was piled so high on tabletops, that barely any light penetrated from the windows. Every surface was layered with old mail, cash register receipts, used movie tickets, art projects, strange ornaments, candleholders, picture frames with no pictures, and all manner of odds and ends. Valuable antiques stood side by side with cheap plastic junk and toys that could have originated inside Happy Meals. But mostly there were books, hundreds of them, their pages jammed with multiple Post-it notes and makeshift bookmarks. Griffin noticed the logo of the Green Hollow Public Library on the spines. It matched the letterhead on many of the pieces of mail — addressed to a Mr. Tobias Fielder and marked OVERDUE NOTIFICATION.

Darren caught Griffin's eye. "We're never going to be able to find anything in here! The FBI couldn't find anything in here!"

"We have to try," Griffin whispered back. Then to

their host, "Uh, Mr. Fielder. How can you be so sure that you didn't misplace that ticket?"

The man took off his macramé cap and hung it on the shiny Winged Victory figure atop a bowling trophy. "This may seem a little messy to you boys, but I know exactly where everything is. I can lay my hand on any of my possessions within a minute. For instance, my original animation cell from Walt Disney's *Fantasia* —" He strode to the dining room table, lifted up a salad spinner, moved aside a stack of magazines, and reached under what looked like a Laundromat bundle of boxer shorts. "Voilà." A small framed cell of Mickey Mouse as the Sorcerer's Apprentice. It was in perfect condition, not even dusty. In fact, despite the total disorder, the house seemed very clean. It was just that Mr. Fielder had never thrown anything away.

Darren was impressed. "You know, that's probably worth a lot of money."

"I'd never sell it," Mr. Fielder told him. "I'm independently wealthy. I quit my job after I won the lottery in 2009. And I've been living exactly the life I want ever since."

"Wait a minute! Back up!" ordered Darren. "You won the lottery?"

Mr. Fielder nodded. "It was a smaller prize than the one you boys are thinking about — a little under four million, and I had to share it with two other winners. The point is it's just not possible for me to forget to check a ticket. Most people are less disciplined because, after all, what's the probability of winning? But me? I know that dreams can come true. I've watched it happen before."

Darren was practically drooling. "Tell me your secrets. What numbers do you play?"

The winner shrugged. "No secrets. I let the machine choose the numbers. I guess somebody up there just liked me that week."

Griffin wandered through the living room, marveling at the organized chaos around him. He looked under a few of the stacks of books, mail, DVDs, newspapers and magazines, vinyl record albums, grocery sacks, cookie sheets, owners' manuals, and award plaques for "salesman of the month." He couldn't see any old lottery tickets lying around. It was all junk, but in Mr. Fielder's mind, it was where it was supposed to be. And anyway, the odds of winning the lottery even once were astronomical. The likelihood that Tobias Fielder had hit the jackpot *again* was so tiny it was off the scale. It just didn't happen.

Eventually, Griffin managed to drag a fascinated Darren away from Mr. Fielder's stories of press conferences and giant cardboard checks. They were tripping their way through the flotsam on the porch when a terrible sight met their eyes.

There were the bikes at the curb. Griffin's was lying in the road.

Luthor was gone.

Where's the mutt?" asked Darren.

"Oh, no!" Griffin groaned. "The leash must have slipped off when he knocked the bike over. Come on, we've got to find him!"

"Don't look at me," said Darren. "That dog hates me."

"He hates everybody! Don't take it personally."

They got back on their bikes and cruised through the streets of Green Hollow.

"Luthor!" bellowed Griffin.

"Just look for terrified people running away from something scary," Darren advised.

"It's no joke!" Griffin exclaimed anxiously. "If we lose that dog, twenty of Luthor wouldn't make up the savage beast we'll have to face when Savannah finds out."

"What's all this 'we' stuff?" Darren snapped back. "It wasn't my idea to bring him on the ticket hunt!"

They traveled the length of the main drag, branching

off onto alternate side streets. Luthor was nowhere to be found. They were almost back to the train station when Darren swung over and grabbed Griffin's arm, nearly pulling him off his bike.

"Bing — look!"

Griffin followed his enemy's pointing finger. Just across the street, a row of gleaming motorcycles was parked outside a glass-front diner.

"He couldn't be in there," Griffin said impatiently. "They wouldn't let a dog in a restaurant."

"Not the mutt," Darren insisted. "The guy on Mike's video — the one who moved last year. The motorcycle guy — Jerry-maybe-Harry."

Griffin pulled up short. Several of the choppers sported the HAWG WILD logo, the same message that their suspect wore on his leather jacket.

Griffin was torn. The plan or the dog. Which came first? He thought of Luthor's long powerful legs. In the time it took to interview these bikers, the Doberman could be in Pennsylvania.

But Jerry/Harry could be here *now*. . . .

"Okay," Griffin said at last. "We see if the guy's there, ask him about the ticket, and then straight back out to search for Luthor."

They turned into the parking lot, leaned their bikes against a mailbox, and started for the restaurant's front door. As they passed the line of parked motorcycles, Darren paused to admire a gleaming

Harley-Davidson on the end. "I'll bet these cost more than some cars!" He reached out and touched the shiny mirror. "It's awesome! Look at the balance of the thing!"

Griffin started to say *Darren, don't!* But it was already too late. Darren gave the chopper a solid shove. The Harley tipped over into the Honda beside it, which in turn knocked over the Kawasaki next in line. One by one, the motorcycles keeled over like dominoes, crashing to the pavement.

A moment later, the diner door flew open and a cascade of bikers poured out, each one bigger than the next, all mad as hornets.

Darren pointed at his companion. "It was him! He did it!"

"I did not!" Griffin squeaked, but his words were lost in the stampede of bikers. *It figures*, he thought, strangely detached from his predicament. *Out of all the risks in my career as a planner, it took Darren Vader to get me killed!*

"You're going to be sorry about this!" grunted the leader in a voice that seemed to emanate from the bowels of the earth.

And then a bark rang out even deeper and more threatening than the voice. A blur of black-and-brown fur flashed onto the scene, putting itself between the bikers and the two cowering boys. Now it was the motorcycle gang that was backing up. It was one thing to be tough. It was quite another to be tough while facing those jaws.

Griffin found his voice at last. "It was an accident! We didn't mean any harm!"

"Call off your monster!" someone shouted.

It was worth a try. "Luthor — it's okay!"

The Doberman backed up a few steps, but maintained his defensive position in front of the boys.

"We're really sorry. We just need to talk to Jerry, or maybe Harry."

There was a confused murmur among the bikers. Finally, one of them said, "You mean Perry?"

Griffin took a hard look and decided that, yes, this was the man from the store's video. "You buy lottery tickets at Mike's Woodstock Market?"

"What's it to you?" Perry demanded.

Griffin told him about their search for the missing ticket. "Mike told us you changed apartments around then. What if you forgot to check those numbers and the ticket got stuffed in a suitcase or box during the move?"

The big bearded man brayed a harsh laugh. "Take it easy, Sherlock. I checked the ticket."

Darren stepped out from behind Griffin. "How can you be sure? It was a year ago."

"I matched three numbers — forty-six bucks. That night, I heard on the news that one ticket won the whole thirty million. So my forty-six bucks stopped looking so good. Yeah, I remember. That kind of thing you don't forget."

Griffin and Darren exchanged a look of frustration. Three suspects. Three dead ends.

And only four days to go.

How's your dad coming along with his allergist?" Savannah asked.

Victor looked blank for a moment, then said, "Oh — uh — pretty good, I guess. The pills weren't working, so they switched him to shots. The doctor says it's a slow process."

"Oh," she replied, disappointed.

He was instantly worried. "Sorry, Savannah. I wish I could take Penelope home so you could get your dog back."

"None of this is Penelope's fault," she said firmly. "Luthor would have needed this tough love sooner or later anyway. I've got no one but myself to blame for that. He's spoiled rotten and I'm the one who did it to him. And who could be angry with Penelope? She's such a joy."

They both watched the cat, who was amusing herself by scrambling up a flight of carpeted stairs and rolling down. Cleopatra was playing, too, but the monkey's heart didn't appear to be in the game today. She seemed listless, her swing at half arc, her bounce all but missing.

"I think your monkey might be sick," Victor ventured, concerned.

Savannah sighed. "She misses Luthor, too. They were inseparable, you know."

Victor did know. Savannah had already told him at least fifteen times.

"I'm not much better," Savannah admitted bleakly. "Last night, I went crawling through the bushes outside Griffin's house. Can you imagine that? Skulking like a ninja on the off chance that I could catch a glimpse of my sweetie." She brightened a little. "Oh, well. One day, all this will be over. Luthor will learn his lesson, and we'll be one big happy family again."

"And my dad's allergies will get better," Victor added helpfully.

Despite Savannah's assurances, he was starting to get an uneasy feeling on his daily visits to the Drysdale house. Victor had done amazingly well since moving to Cedarville. After the bullying he'd endured at his old school, this town and these friends meant the world to him.

Yet he couldn't escape the feeling that the whole situation was on shaky ground. His passport to this new life had been stamped when Savannah had taken in Penelope. Not that Savannah, Pitch, Logan, Melissa, and Ben were so shallow that they'd turn their backs on him over a cat. Still, it was time to find something else that would cement his position within the group. But what? Another animal wouldn't work.

Whatever it took, he had to find a way to make it happen. These new friends were too important to him — especially after what he'd been through in Bass Junction.

He was on his way home, his head swimming with these thoughts, when Darren Vader stopped him on Honeybee Street.

Although the two had barely spoken before, Victor felt an instant connection. Both had been victims of cruel bullying, so there was an unbreakable bond between them. And Victor was full of admiration for the way Darren had stood up in front of the entire school and faced down his tormentor, Griffin Bing.

"Hey, Victor, how's it going?"

"Pretty good. How about you?" Victor replied. Then he added cautiously, "Any more problems with Griffin?"

"Forget him," Darren scoffed. "You know what? I actually think he did me a favor."

Victor made a face. "I don't see how pushing you around could qualify as that."

The story Darren told was a real eye-opener. Until then, Victor had not known the full details of the hoax that had sent Darren sifting through garbage all over town. But the goal of that search — the unclaimed thirty-million-dollar jackpot — was one hundred percent real! Darren had taken Griffin's bullying and turned it into something *positive*! He'd interviewed the owner of the store, examined his security video for last October 6, and even created a list of possible purchasers of the missing ticket.

"I just *know* I can find it," Darren finished. "But the time is running short, and I'm only one guy. If only I had some help — just a few more people — I'm sure I could bring a lot of happiness into somebody's life. And I'll bet that big winner would give us a reward, too."

At that moment, Victor understood exactly what he had to do to solidify his position with his new friends. How many times had they referred to Griffin as The Man With The Plan? That's what he needed — a plan for them to carry out together. And Darren had just given him one. Even if they never got anywhere near this legendary Giga-Millions ticket, working toward a common purpose would be worth fifty cats living at the Drysdales'.

A plan! Why hadn't he thought of that?

"Let's talk to the others," Victor urged. "I know they'll be anxious to get in on this."

"There's a problem," Darren admitted. "Those guys don't trust me."

Victor was mystified. "Why wouldn't they trust you?"

"It's Griffin's fault. He's been bad-mouthing me since we were in diapers. They hate me because he hates me. I never even had a chance with them."

Victor, who knew what that felt like, was instantly

sympathetic. "We can fix it. *I* can fix it. They're really nice kids. If we explain things, I'm positive they'll see the light."

Darren shook his head sadly. "There's no time to work all that out. We've only got four days before the ticket expires." He put on a brave smile. "Thanks for trying, man."

"We can still do it," Victor insisted. "You'll be a totally silent partner. I'll tell everybody the whole thing is my idea."

Darren had tears in his eyes. "You'd do that for me?"

"Totally. And when it's over, we'll set the record straight. They're great guys, but they've got a blind spot when it comes to Griffin Bing. We'll give them a chance to get to know the real you."

Victor took stock of himself. A new friend, the perfect plan, a black mark against Griffin, and — who knew — maybe even thirty million dollars.

This had been a good day.

22

The sight had become a familiar one, even to Ferret Face — Melissa, hunched over the computer in her room, working her technological magic for a plan. The little creature peered out of Ben's sleeve, watching alongside the team as the shy girl expertly guided her fingers across the keyboard.

It had taken the tech whiz no more than thirty seconds to access the security camera footage from Mike's Woodstock Market on her laptop. Now a procession of head shots flickered on the screen at breakneck speed — thousands of them, flashing one after the other.

"I've created some new facial recognition software," she explained from behind the curtain of stringy hair. "The program is comparing the people from the security camera to the images on the DMV database."

"DMV?" Victor echoed.

"Department of Motor Vehicles. I hacked into their mainframe. These are all the driver's license photos in

New York State. It isn't foolproof," she added apologetically. "If the winning ticket was bought by somebody out of state, we won't be able to identify him or her."

"Shame on you," Pitch said sarcastically. "That kind of carelessness could get you kicked out of evil genius school."

At that moment, Melissa's printer whirred to life. The team gathered around as it spat out three pages of names and addresses.

"This is awesome!" Victor breathed in genuine admiration. "Melissa, you rock!"

Ben bit his lip. Maybe Victor was blown away by Melissa's talents, but nobody else was. How many times had the team witnessed Melissa's electronic miracles? Maybe that explained the bad taste in Ben's mouth. *Team* meant *Griffin's* team, and Griffin was not around to be a part of this. It didn't feel right.

Victor was fine. Victor was *great*. Meeting new people and making new friends was a good thing, wasn't it? Of course it was!

"All right." Victor examined the list. "Here's what we're going to do. . . ."

For Ben, that was the problem. This was a *plan*. The search for a thirty-million-dollar lottery ticket! Griffin lived for stuff like this. How could they leave him out of it?

Ben caught himself rubbernecking out Melissa's second-story window, peering in the direction of the

Bing home three blocks over. Savannah was doing it, too. For sure she was thinking of Luthor.

The team without Griffin; Savannah without Luthor; Vader at Griffin's side.

The whole universe was out of whack.

The Doberman hunkered down just outside the garage, watching intently as Griffin's father tinkered with his invention.

"You know," Mr. Bing commented, "I always thought Luthor was a big, dumb mutt, but he's really smart. Look how interested he is in my work. He can sit and watch me for hours."

"Yeah, Dad." Griffin had a theory about that. Luthor wasn't fascinated by the SweetPick — he was scared to death of it. Every time the U-Bundle mechanism lashed out, he would jump back, and the hiss of the slicing Safe-chete blade raised hackles on the back of his neck. All walks began with a nervous bark over his shoulder at the closed garage door. And when Mr. Bing invited him into the workshop for a closer look, the Doberman refused to budge. The reason Luthor wouldn't take his eyes off the device was that he was convinced it was coming to get him.

There had been interest in the SweetPick from Brazil. Mr. Bing was currently resizing the harness to match the height of the South American crop, using his son as a typical worker. It was a tricky process that left Griffin wearing the prototype for hours on end while his father fiddled, measured, and ordered parts. Most of the time, Griffin felt like a store mannequin — although he had to admit he'd never gotten so much respect from Luthor as when he was wearing the Dangerous Thing.

"Is that your dad's new whatchamacallit?"

Griffin turned to see Ben standing before him on the driveway.

"I'm helping my dad," Griffin grumbled. "He'll be back any minute. What do you want?"

Ben shrugged. "Just figured I'd come by. Ferret Face misses you."

Griffin took note of the unmoving lump inside Ben's shirt. "He looks really excited to see me again."

"Maybe he doesn't recognize you in that gizmo. Listen, Griffin, the team has something going on, and we thought you might want to get in on it."

Griffin's eyes narrowed. "You mean a plan?"

"Not a plan," Ben said quickly. "It's more like an activity that everybody's doing. You know, for a purpose."

"That's a plan!" Griffin exclaimed. "I'll bet it's Victor's plan, isn't it?"

"Well, maybe. But —"

"Then what do you need me for?" Griffin cut him off. "You've got the *new* Man With The Plan!"

"Come on, Griffin," Ben wheedled. "This can't be fun for you, either. Fighting with everybody, babysitting Luthor, hanging out with Vader."

"Go back to Victor and your brilliant plan. I've got a little something going myself. And, no, you're not invited to be part of it."

Luthor let out a threatening growl, which had Ben retreating to the sidewalk and home. "Well, if you change your mind . . ."

"I won't." Griffin reached out to pat the Doberman. "Thanks, pal."

Luthor backed away from the SweetPick on Griffin's chest.

Griffin frowned, his lips forming a thin line. What kind of plan could that guy Victor have? Something useless, probably, like raking leaves.

But he had to admit that Operation Jackpot wasn't exactly cruising, either. Darren, the coward, wasn't returning Griffin's phone calls. One little motorcycle gang, and he was spooked.

The clock was ticking, and there were still forty-four people on the suspect list.

He had to face the fact that Darren was blowing him off.

If this plan was going to have any chance of working, Griffin would have to forge on alone.

23

Victor regarded Logan in perplexity. The boy had halted halfway up the house's front walk and now stood frozen in concentration.

"Logan, are you okay?"

"Shhhh!" Logan hissed. "I'm *preparing*."

"Preparing what?"

"Getting into character," the young actor explained. "I'm going to create a role so vivid, so believable that those people will never realize we're just a regular couple of kids. Maybe I'm a researcher, working for Giga-Millions, doing a study on how long people keep their old tickets."

"That could work," Victor said diplomatically. "Or maybe we could just tell them the truth — we know they bought the right kind of ticket from the right store on the right day and we're worried that they might be missing out on a big prize."

"That isn't very dramatic," Logan pointed out.

"It could be," Victor reasoned. "Can you imagine some lady finding a thirty-million-dollar ticket in her junk drawer?"

"That would be life-changing," Logan agreed, warming to the idea. "Like reality TV. Sometimes the greatest acting is just being yourself."

Two blocks to the east, Savannah and Melissa were approaching the second address on the list. Savannah carried Penelope in her arms. "You'll see," she promised. "People are much friendlier when you have an animal with you."

And it worked. The first words out of Mrs. Alastair's mouth were "What a lovely cat!"

In no time at all, Penelope was lapping at a saucer of milk, and Savannah was explaining about the missing lottery ticket and the huge prize that was set to expire. Melissa was content to let her partner do all the talking. She was much more comfortable interacting with a computer than with actual humans.

Mrs. Alastair listened patiently and then said, "That's lovely, dear, but I'm not your big winner."

"How can you be sure?" Savannah pressed. "It was almost a year ago."

In answer, Mrs. Alastair led them through the neat house to an unused bedroom at the rear. The girls stared. The room was crisscrossed with old-fashioned clothesline. Each pin — and there were hundreds — held a ticket. The lines were marked by lottery name —

Lotto, Powerball, Giga-Millions. She went straight to October and found the October 6 drawing. "I keep these," she explained, "so I never have to worry that an unclaimed prize might be mine. You see?" She handed the small slip to Savannah. "Not a single number. Just my luck."

Not far away, Pitch took notice when the name Amelia Alastair was erased from the master list on her phone.

"Another one bites the dust," she commented. "And Mr. de Palma comes off, too. That makes it — eleven down, thirty-six to go."

"I've got flat feet," Ben complained. "And my butt hurts. My bike seat wasn't meant to carry me to Green Hollow every day after school."

"Thirty millions bucks buys a lot of bike seats," Pitch assured him. "You can get a gold-plated one."

Ben made a face. "If we'd found that ticket in the pocket of Mr. de Palma's old bathrobe, the money would be his, not ours."

Pitch shrugged. "Maybe we'll get a reward or a finder's fee."

"Maybe!" Ben spat with such disgust that Ferret Face came up to investigate the disturbance. "Can you imagine Griffin basing an operation on *maybe*? The whole point of planning is that you know for sure!"

Pitch nodded sympathetically. "I miss him, too, you know. We all do. But remember, nobody kicked him out, not even Victor. He kicked himself out."

Ben had no answer. It was the plain, unvarnished truth. It was Griffin's own stubbornness that had caused this terrible rift. The same strength of character that enabled him to push a plan through to fruition by sheer force of will also made him a mule.

In a weird way, The Man With The Plan cast a larger shadow in his absence than when he was actually there. Walking up to the houses on the suspect list, Ben's first thought was always *How would Griffin approach this?* Griffin seemed to be looking out at him from the family portraits that hung in the houses they visited. A couple of times, he was positive he'd seen Griffin's bike sail by on the street — as if his friend had nothing better to do than ride around Green Hollow.

"Okay, next house," said Pitch, consulting her phone. "Forty-four Spruce Lane."

"Let's go," sighed Ben.

Kid, I wasn't born yesterday," the man told Griffin. "As soon as I heard how much money was at stake, I checked my storage locker. I went through the glove compartment of my car, and all the pockets of all my jackets. I even went through my wife's handbags, and let me tell you, that's more debris than gets kicked up by a tsunami. And you know what the answer is? Whoever that missing winner is, he's not me."

"I know you think you searched everywhere," Griffin pressed, "but sometimes a fresh pair of eyes can spot something you might not notice because you know your own stuff too well."

The man shook his head in exasperation. "Why can't you kids just sell candy bars, like in the old days? The other one drove me crazy, too — 'Did you check the crawl space, did you check the septic tank, did you check the underwear drawer?'"

"The other one?" Griffin was instantly alert. "Someone else was asking about the ticket?"

"Yeah, about half an hour ago. Another kid your age, same nosy questions, also trying to make me rich."

"Can you describe him?" Griffin persisted.

"Did it ever occur to you that I don't like being reminded that I bought a ticket on the right day from the right place, but I can't remember whether I checked it or not? I probably did — I always used to. But it's something you don't like to think about — especially when a new kid comes every half hour to bug you. Now please go away."

Shut out on the front porch with the door slammed behind him, The Man With The Plan took a single piece of information from the man's rant: Somebody else was asking about the ticket.

It could be only one person: Darren Vader. He hadn't given up on the plan. He was going solo so he wouldn't have to split the reward money!

In an instant, Griffin was back on his bike, pedaling toward town and Mike's Woodstock Market. "Mike! Mike!" he exclaimed, bursting into the store.

The tall, thin hippie storekeeper was behind the counter, finishing up with a customer. "Would you like some aromatherapy candles to go with that?" he inquired.

The woman stared at him. "With Band-Aids?"

"Serenity heals better than any medicine," Mike lectured. "At Woodstock, there were babies born with nothing more than rainwater and paper towels. But there was spiritual energy everywhere."

The customer left hurriedly, and Mike turned his attention to Griffin. "What can I do for you, man?"

"Remember Darren?" Griffin asked. "The kid who was with me the first time I came in here?"

"Sure," the storekeeper replied. "I just watched the video of that visit. Ever since you showed me how to access the footage from my security camera, I've been kind of hooked on it. You know, I think Mick Jagger might have come in here once to buy Maalox. I can't believe I didn't recognize him."

"But have you seen him in person?" Griffin probed. "Darren, I mean — not Mick Jagger."

Mike shook his shaggy head. "Not since the day you young dudes came in together and taught me to watch the video. It's a groovy way to pass the downtime. Want to check it out?"

"Maybe later," Griffin acknowledged absently. He understood that Operation Jackpot had just been transformed in a fundamental way. The ticking clock was no longer his only enemy.

If Griffin had accepted Mike's invitation to view the security video on the computer, he would have seen something that would have shocked him to his core — Victor Phoenix, leading Pitch, Savannah, Logan, Melissa, and Ben into the market to stock up on drinks for the ticket hunt.

Time stamp: barely an hour ago.

*   *   *

Darren Vader polished off the last huge bite of his breakfast burrito and tossed the greasy wrapper to the floor, in spite of the fact that there was a trash can barely a foot away. "It's good for the tiles," he offered to a group of seventh-grade girls who were passing by.

At peace with the world, he strolled up to his locker, fed in the combination, and opened the door. A sheet of paper floated down and landed at his feet.

I'm onto you. I know every sleazy thing you're doing, and I don't know why I'm surprised. Sleaze is your middle name. Let me tell you something. I don't need your help to find that ticket. I'm really close. And I'm going to make it my mission in life to see to it that none of that reward money ever falls into your slimy hands. Not one thin dime. That's a promise.

It was unsigned, but the handwriting was unmistakably that of Griffin Bing.

Darren's first instinct was to panic. How could Griffin possibly have found out that Darren had recruited Victor and the team to join the search? That would have taken not one but two blabbermouths — first Victor would have had to blab to the others that Darren was his silent partner. And second, one of them would have had to blab *that* to Griffin. It was possible, but not very likely. The odds were that Griffin didn't have the whole picture.

Yet, with a sinking heart, Darren realized that it didn't matter how wrong Griffin happened to be. He was mad, and he was close, which meant he would make good on his threat to keep Darren from profiting from the missing ticket.

The thought of all that money floating around, and none of it sticking to him, made Darren's burrito turn to stone in his stomach.

He caught up with Victor in the east stairwell outside the science lab.

"Oh, hi, Darren. How's it going?"

Darren waited for the stairwell to clear out. "How's the search coming?" he asked finally.

"Pretty well," Victor replied. "We've checked almost all the names on Melissa's list, but so far, no luck."

"What do you mean, 'no luck'?" Darren demanded. "What's luck got to do with it? This is supposed to be scientific! We've got every person who bought a ticket on that day! Sooner or later, the right guy has to come up!"

Victor Phoenix felt a nagging sense that he had been down this road before. Darren was right up in his face, and his tone was forceful and unpleasant.

"Well," Victor began, "there are a few addresses that we've hit but we couldn't find anyone home. And, of course, there's always the real possibility that the ticket just doesn't exist anymore —"

"No, man!" Darren cut him off. "You're thinking like a loser! The ticket is out there — I can *taste* it! And we've only got two days left!"

Victor backed up a step, and found himself pressed against the banister. The déjà vu was undeniable. He might as well have been back at Bass Junction, getting harassed and intimidated. This was not what he expected from Darren, who'd made an impassioned speech about bullying on one of Victor's first days in Cedarville. This was not what he expected from the boy who'd stood up to Griffin Bing.

Maybe he'd been wrong to trust Darren. Maybe things in Cedarville were not what they seemed.

25

Twenty-four hours to go.

The rules were fair, Melissa reflected. A year to cash in a lottery ticket. Who could possibly need longer than that?

Yet tomorrow, at six p.m., nearly thirty million dollars would turn to dust.

It was more than just a big number. It was a dream home, a college education, a trip around the world — and not just for one person, but for whole families, and for generations to come. It could be devoted to a worthy cause, like a major donation to charity. It could buy a Maserati for someone who was keeping an old clunker alive on a wing and a prayer. It could purchase life-saving surgery, or be used to fill Madison Square Garden with peanut brittle. In the end, it didn't matter if it would be spent wisely or frittered away on nonsense. It belonged to somebody, and it was going to waste.

All these thoughts whirled through Melissa's head as she sat in stiff-necked misery, in her least comfortable dress, trying to enjoy Aunt Chrisoula's roast lamb. Here it was, the next to last day, and was she in Green Hollow with Victor and the team? No, she was at a birthday party for a seventy-nine-year-old lady who barely spoke English.

Thanks to Melissa's facial recognition software, they had a name and address for every Giga-Millions customer on the video from Mike's Woodstock Market. But that had left them with too many suspects, and not enough time to check them out. Now they were down to the wire, with fourteen names still on the list. Would the clock run out on them?

She could be sure of only one thing: Her place was on the search with the others.

They needed Griffin. Victor was a great guy, but he wasn't The Man With The Plan. No one was. Griffin had come up with some harebrained schemes before, but never once had he let a plan crash and burn.

How could they ever have turned their backs on him?

"Melissa, what have you got there?" Mr. Dukakis asked irritably.

"Nothing, Dad."

Her mother emitted a long-suffering sigh. "Oh, I don't think it's nothing. You've got your phone hidden in your napkin. I don't suppose it would help if I told you that there's a real world that exists outside of cyberspace."

Okay, she was caught. But how else was she going to keep track of the progress of the search? She'd created this app for all the team members so that, when a suspect was eliminated, the list would be shortened for everyone.

"I'll turn it off, Mom." She meant it. But she didn't say when.

As the family sang "Happy Birthday" to Aunt Chrisoula, Victor texted to say they were packing it in for the night. Tomorrow was expiration day, and the app still showed eleven names.

Yet it was the weekend, so the team planned an all-out last-ditch effort.

There might still be time.

For Darren, October 6 dawned like the day of his own funeral.

The instant he woke up and looked at the clock, he calculated the minutes to Zero Hour. And it really was Zero Hour — the moment when all that money became zero. 7:28 a.m. That meant — he calculated furiously — 632 minutes to go.

No, 631. He'd wasted a precious minute doing the math.

"I made your favorite for breakfast," his mother greeted him as he hauled himself downstairs. "Silver dollar pancakes."

"I hate them!" he snapped, picturing thirty million of the things. "I never want them again!"

He couldn't think about money. And that was a problem, because money was what he thought about all the time.

Eleven names to go . . .

No, don't get your hopes up! The letdown would tear open his soul. Especially if Bing got the money, and Darren didn't —

Not possible! The world could never be so cruel!

The TV was set on the Game Show Network — people trying to win money! He hurled the remote across the room.

"I need to run to the bank," his father said. "Want to come along for the ride?"

"Oh, no!" Darren groaned. "No! No! Please, no!"

"What's with you?" Mr. Vader demanded. "I'm just going to get some cash."

Darren wheeled away from his father and stumbled back upstairs. Once in his room, he did what he had promised himself he would not do — he checked the app Melissa had created to track the search for the ticket. What? He counted the names again. Ten! That meant the team was out there bright and early, and they had eliminated another suspect!

If they've made this much progress already . . .

Stop it! he exhorted himself. He couldn't drive himself crazy with pipe dreams of money he would never possess.

Yet, as the day went on, the phone kept beckoning. By lunchtime, only eight names remained on the list. By two o'clock, it was down to five.

Five! He couldn't believe his eyes as he stared at the small screen. This changed everything! Victor and those boneheads were too dumb to know it couldn't be done, and they were *doing* it!

I've got to get in on this!

How Darren managed to make it to Green Hollow on his bike without killing himself would forever stand as one of life's miracles. In spite of all safety rules, he kept checking the app, pedaling without looking. When the count went down to four suspects, he rear-ended a Nassau County bus, and very nearly blew a tire against its bumper. When it hit three, he jumped the curb and wiped out in a field of ragweed. But not even the spasms of sneezing put an end to his frantic journey.

When the remaining names dwindled to two, he was already inside the Green Hollow town limits. He dropped his phone and cracked the screen by stepping on it when he stooped to retrieve it. The damage barely registered with him. In his mind he was buying a hundred new ones.

Two suspects. It had to be one or the other. The possibility that neither had the ticket was too horrible for him to contemplate. Nothing could be that unfair. For more than thirteen years, Darren Vader had waited to strike it rich. This had to be his moment.

He stashed his battered bike in the rack at the Green Hollow train station and made for Mike's Woodstock Market. As he ran, he checked the app one final time, which nearly caused him to collide with a No Parking sign. What he saw on the cracked monitor very nearly put his fluttering heart into cardiac arrest.

Victor and the team had done it! They had narrowed the search down to a single name.

Grant Bruckman, 214 Kiwi Lane.

He could have kissed Victor Phoenix right then, and even Pitch, Savannah, Logan, Melissa, and Ben. Sure, they were Bing's ex-posse, and probably hated Darren a lot. But they'd really come through this time. And thirty million bucks bought a lot of forgiveness.

Well, they had served their purpose, and they were out of it now. There was a big prize to be had, and Darren intended to have it all.

The problem was those guys were probably already pedaling for Kiwi Lane, wherever that was. They had a big head start, and the only way to beat them to the punch was with a car. There were no two ways about it — he needed an adult.

He burst into the market. "Mike! Mike!" He stared at the teenage girl behind the cash register. "Where's Mike! Don't tell me he isn't here!"

She snapped her gum and pointed to the back of the store, where the lanky shopkeeper was stacking boxes of diapers. He glanced up at Darren. "There you are. The other young dude was looking for you."

"Never mind that!" Darren rasped. "I know who has the ticket! You need to drive me before somebody else gets there first!"

Mike continued to work on his pyramid of Pampers. "That's really not my thing, man. Money just messes with your head. Look at yourself. It's harshing your whole view of the universe."

"The sixties ended a long time ago," Darren pleaded. "People *like* money now. This jackpot could change your life — you wouldn't have to work in the store all day!"

"The store keeps me close to my fellow man," Mike informed him.

"You could retire and hang out with your fellow man all day! With flowers in your hair!"

The storekeeper piled infant size at the top of the stack.

"You could buy your own farm and live off the land and grow organic flax while listening to the Beatles! Or you could move to San Francisco and groove or something!" Darren was babbling now, frantically trying to get through to this laid-back hippie. His eyes scoured the store. There had to be something here that would penetrate all that hair and the thick skull underneath it — that would upend his desire to have nothing and want less!

And there it was, right next to the register — the instant-coffee jar with the slit in its lid. Darren stared at the hand-lettered sign: GIVE TO THE CREATION OF A WOODSTOCK MUSIC FESTIVAL NATIONAL HISTORIC SITE. It seemed to hold no more than the few coins that had been there the first time Darren had entered the store.

"Or," he finished triumphantly, "you could donate the money to make Woodstock a national historic site."

The storekeeper turned around, creating a breeze that billowed his poncho. "You think?"

"Totally! That's the great thing about money — you spend it on what *you* want!"

The exposed portion of Mike's face grew dreamy. "Future generations will be able to see what we were doing there! That we weren't just partying in the mud — that we were pooling our own psychic energy to create an example of how humanity could be!"

"But we've got to hurry," Darren added urgently. "If somebody else gets there first, you can kiss that historic site good-bye!"

Galvanized into action, Mike grabbed a set of keys from a hook. "Mind the store!" he tossed over his shoulder to the clerk. "I have urgent business!" He dashed out the door, with Darren scrambling to keep up with his long-legged strides.

26

OPERATION JACKPOT—THE FINAL HOURS

(i) . . .

G riffin stared at the paper. What was there to say about a plan that was going down the drain? He wished he could blame it all on Darren's desertion . . . but that wasn't it.

I was too eager to make it happen, he admitted to himself. *I wanted to prove to Ben and the others that there's only one Man With The Plan.*

At this awful moment — watching the plan founder — what Griffin really felt was *lonely*. Failing was bad enough, but to have no one there to say "That's okay, buddy. You gave it your best shot" had to be rock bottom. At that moment, he missed his team more than he resented Victor Phoenix. Now he wondered if there had been too much bad blood, too many angry words, for things ever to be the same again. If that were true, even coming up with the ticket and getting all thirty million dollars for himself wouldn't be worth it.

Anyway, ticket finding was out of the question now because he wasn't even in Green Hollow looking for it. Dad had finished designing the smaller SweetPick harness and had asked Griffin to help him test it. Griffin couldn't very well refuse. His father's meeting with the Brazilians had been pushed up, so this weekend would be the last chance to iron out any bugs.

Mom wasn't around, which meant Luthor had to be included in this expedition. Coaxing him into the station wagon was never easy. Getting him to stay there when Dad loaded the SweetPick in the back took all they had left of the Puppy Treats Savannah had brought over.

"I hope the Brazilians place a large enough order to pay for all the dog food this is costing," muttered Mr. Bing, putting the car in gear.

The testing ground turned out to be an open field lined with transformer towers east of Cedarville along the Green Hollow town line. There was no sugarcane, obviously. But the tall reeds, weeds, and grass provided a similar environment in which to put the SweetPick through its paces.

The device was lighter than before, especially with the modified harness, which was now a more comfortable fit.

"That's good news," Mr. Bing decided. "In South America, they use younger workers, and a lot of women, too. So you're a better model than I'd be, sizewise."

Luthor refused to leave the car, but his nose hung out the open rear window as he kept a wary eye on the Dangerous Thing.

Following his father's instructions, Griffin cut and bundled grass, rushes, and even a stand of wild rhubarb. The prototype was performing beautifully, until there was a sharp snap, and one of the bolts that held the Safe-chete blade in place sung past Dad's ear, disappearing into the weeds.

After much searching, Mr. Bing came up with it. "Stripped!" he announced in disgust. "Wouldn't you know it? I've got half my workshop in the car, but I didn't bring another bolt."

So Dad drove to the nearest hardware store while Griffin and Luthor cooled their heels in the shadow of the transformers in their test field. The detached Safe-chete blade lay on the grass, but that made the Doberman no more comfortable. He kept a safe distance, never taking his attention off the SweetPick. Griffin had to laugh, because Luthor's naked fear reminded him of his own feelings toward the Doberman.

Griffin pointed to the blade on the ground. "It can't slice and dice you now; it can only tie you up."

The roar of a loud engine swelled in the field. Griffin watched the road, expecting to see a huge truck pulling at least two trailers. Instead, a strange vehicle came into view. It was a 1969 Volkswagen bus with its original motor and no muffler, gloriously painted with peace signs and psychedelic colors. Even before he spotted the driver, Griffin knew who it had to be. Mike hunched over the wheel, his FLOWER POWER headband as vivid as the Day-Glo rainbows on his van.

There was someone with him in the passenger seat. Griffin squinted. Piggy eyes, cement head . . .

"Vader!" he exclaimed aloud, his blood boiling. He should have known! That money-grubbing slimeball would never give up on thirty million dollars. Even after the deadline had passed, he'd be booking passage on a spaceship so he could run himself through a time warp and get a second chance. Vader must have gotten an eleventh-hour lead on the missing ticket. And he'd somehow convinced the last hippie on Long Island to give up all his 1960s idealism and make a sprint for the cash.

Griffin wasn't aware of the moment he started running, but he was at full speed by the time the VW flashed by on the side road. He didn't consider the long odds against catching a motor vehicle. He barely noticed that he was still wearing the SweetPick prototype, or that the Safe-chete blade was lying abandoned on the grass like a piece of junk. He just ran.

A few seconds later, a large black-and-tan blur overtook him on the left. Luthor would never pass up an opportunity to chase a car, especially when his human companion was chasing it, too. And knowing that the

SweetPick was back there behind him lent wings to his four muscular legs.

"Good boy, Luthor!" Griffin panted. "Stick with him!" Griffin might lose the car, but Luthor never would.

The road traced the boundary between Green Hollow and another suburban town, Swandon. Even hustling at top speed, Griffin fell behind quickly, and soon the van disappeared from view. He could still see the Doberman, a tiny dot in the distance. Less than a minute later, even the dog was gone.

The doubts came then. *What am I doing? How could I be so stupid? I took off on Dad, abandoned the Safe-chete blade, lost Luthor, and I'll never catch Vader now!*

He was about to slink back to the testing ground, when a speck reappeared on the horizon, assuming canine dimensions as it grew closer. Luthor was starting back. That meant the van had stopped and the Doberman was returning to pick up Griffin and lead him to it.

Griffin usually rolled his eyes at Savannah's lectures on the brilliance of her sweetie, but he had to admit this was Luthor's finest hour. His brain had figured out what needed to be done, and he was doing it. Now he loped over to Griffin, ignoring his terror of the SweetPick. Lassie herself, Griffin was sure, would have been incapable of such loyalty, resourcefulness, and courage.

"Luthor, you're the best!" Griffin wanted to hug the Doberman but remembered at the last moment that he was still wearing the SweetPick. It would be unkind to test the boundaries of such bravery. Instead, he said, "There's a big steak in this for you, buddy," and the dog began to lead the way back along the road.

Swandon was farther from the train line, making it smaller and less a commuter town than either Cedarville or Green Hollow. Its most prominent feature was Swandon College, a cluster of ivy-covered redbrick buildings on a treelined campus.

Of course! thought Griffin. There was no business district in Swandon. People had to go to Green Hollow or Cedarville for restaurants or movie theaters or stores. The closest place to buy a lottery ticket was Mike's. The winner could just as easily be here as in Green Hollow.

Griffin wished he'd gone out for the track team. A little extra stamina would have come in handy on the long jog into Swandon — especially with the SweetPick weighing him down. He was about ready to pass out when he spotted the van parked in front of what looked like a gracious old Victorian home. Seeing the finish line within reach gave him the second wind he needed, and he and Luthor trotted up the circular drive and stood panting in front of the entranceway.

At close range, the place looked a lot more run-down, with loose shutters and peeling paint. Three

Greek letters painted across the double doors declared this to be Sigma Delta Phi.

A fraternity house! Griffin's heart sank. There could be twenty or thirty frat brothers living in there! Instinctively, he plugged this new information into the plan. On the one hand, it would be harder to find the owner of the ticket. On the other, Darren would have to deal with that complication, too, which might give Griffin the chance to catch up.

Heavy pounding hip-hop bass resounded from the house, even though all the windows were closed. These fraternity guys sure liked their music loud. Griffin could only imagine the kind of stereo they'd buy when one of them realized he'd just won thirty million bucks.

Griffin knocked on the door and, when nobody answered, kicked at it. "Anybody home?" he bellowed. At last, he barged in uninvited, and froze, mouth dropping open in amazement. A massive party was in full swing. Wall-to-wall revelers packed the house, gyrated on the dance floor, mobbed the food table, and spilled up the spiral staircase to the second story. The stereo was blasting so loud that Griffin *felt* the music as much as he heard it — the air actually moved with the pulsing beat.

A mountain of a fraternity brother in a Sigma Delta Phi T-shirt that strained to contain his overdeveloped muscles barred Griffin's entry. "This is a private party, kid, not Chuck E. Cheese."

Sticking to the plan, Griffin faced him down. "Did you buy a Giga-Millions ticket last October sixth?"

"I said get lost!" He reached for Griffin, intending to toss him out the way he'd come in.

Griffin stepped aside to reveal Luthor at the end of his leash. His single warning bark could be heard even over the roar of the music.

The bodybuilder backed away to admit the newcomers. "You know you got your knapsack on backward."

Griffin stayed on message. "Is there anybody here who buys lottery tickets?"

But the frat boy had melted into the crowd, far from Luthor's path.

Griffin scanned the rocking house for Darren's sturdy form or a tall figure topped with Mike's flyaway hair. It was like searching for a needle in a haystack. There must have been two hundred people packed in like sardines.

How was he ever going to find the right person in this *Where's Waldo?* of college kids?

27

Darren, too, was lost in the sea of partygoers, trapped in the kitchen behind a conga line of seven frat brothers who had duct-taped themselves together at the waist. He had one advantage over Griffin, though — a name.

"Is one of you guys Grant Bruckman?" he shouted above the din.

A high-kicking sneaker nearly took his head off, and he had to duck.

Mike had his hands over his ears. "They call this music?"

"It's pretty loud!" Darren agreed.

"I don't mind loud!" Mike insisted. "I was at Woodstock! But this is garbage! Haven't these kids heard of the Beatles? Joni Mitchell? Simon and Garfunkel?"

Darren approached the conga line from the rear, safe from the flying feet. "Grant Bruckman?" he rasped again.

One of them pointed to the living room, which wasn't much help. It was a solid mass of jumping, dancing humanity. You couldn't fit a toothpick between the people.

He dragged Mike past the conga line and through the doorway into the giant double parlor. Swinging arms beat at them as they fought their way through the mob.

The storekeeper was still complaining. "In the sixties, we sang about love, peace, and social justice! These songs can't change the world! I'll bet you can't even play them backward to find the hidden message!"

Darren ignored him. *"Grant!"* he hollered. *"Grant Bruckman! Are you here?"* His voice disappeared in the general noise.

Then something completely unexpected happened. The crush of dancers parted like the Red Sea, but there seemed to be nothing in the gap that was created. Darren lowered his gaze and spotted the cause of the disruption: an all-too-familiar snout and a canine expression that clearly said, *Get out of my way.*

Darren jumped. It was Luthor. And, handling the leash a couple of steps behind the Doberman, Griffin Bing.

Darren fled back into the kitchen and hid behind a butcher block. How had Bing found the frat house? He couldn't possibly know about Melissa's app!

It doesn't matter how he got here, Darren reminded himself. *He's here, which makes it twice as urgent to identify Bruckman and grab the ticket.*

He still had an edge over Griffin — Mike, and a quick ride to the lottery office in his hippie-mobile.

He looked around. Mike was nowhere to be seen.

The station wagon jumped the curb and stopped a few feet into the weeds.

"You wouldn't believe how hard it is to find a hardware store around here," complained Mr. Bing, trudging across the field to the testing area. "And when you do find one, they've got every size bolt except the one you need. Which means you need another store —"

His voice trailed off with the slow realization that he wasn't getting an answer. "Griffin?"

Silence.

"What happened? Did you doze off?"

In growing alarm, he realized that maybe Griffin could sleep through his return, but no one could ever sneak up on Luthor. The guard-dog training was too firmly ingrained.

"All right, Griffin. This isn't funny anymore. You can come out now."

A glimpse of something shiny caught his eye. He reached down into the reeds and grass and pulled up the detached Safe-chete blade. There was no sign of the rest of the SweetPick. Griffin must still be wearing the body pack.

But where?

*   *   *

Six bikes rolled up to 214 Kiwi Lane.

Savannah stroked Penelope's soft fur as the cat relaxed in the basket in front of her handlebars. "What is this place?"

Victor took in the big home with the Greek letters on the door. "I think it's one of the fraternities at Swandon College. Grant Bruckman must be a student."

Pitch hopped down and started for the front door. "Sounds like they're having a party. Cool. I've heard frat parties are wild."

"We're not here to party," Ben reminded her, repositioning Ferret Face inside his shirt. "We need to get the ticket from Grant and head straight to the lottery office. It's almost four."

"I don't like parties," came Melissa's soft voice from behind her hair.

"We'll do all the talking," Victor assured her. "Let's go."

The blond boy was halfway up the front walk when the door was flung wide and three frat brothers backed out of the house, carrying an armchair with a partygoer draped over it, fast asleep. A second face had been drawn on his high forehead in shaving cream. The three planted the chair on the lawn and raced back inside.

Pitch grinned. "What did I tell you? Wild."

"You say that like it's something good," mumbled Melissa.

They were about to enter when the bodybuilder

blocked their way. He regarded the six middle schoolers suspiciously. "You don't have a dog, do you?"

"We've got a cat," offered Savannah, holding out Penelope. "Isn't she beautiful?"

"Unless you've got a panther, beat it."

Slam!

"Now what?" asked Ben, comforting Ferret Face, who didn't like confrontation.

"You can't just walk into a frat house at our age," clucked Logan. "It takes *acting*. You have to create a character who *belongs* there."

"I'm four foot nine," Ben protested. "What am I supposed to do — stilt-walk?"

"Haven't you ever heard of those supergenius kids who get into college when they're eleven?" Logan exclaimed, inspired. "Just give me a minute to get into character."

"If you can convince people you're a genius," Ben said, "then you *are* a great actor."

There was a whistle from above. "Guys — up here."

Everybody stared. Pitch mugged down at them from a second-story balcony. "Climb up the trellis like I did. I'll help you over the rail."

There was a chorus of protest. It was a small matter for Pitch to ascend the wooden framework. She'd been born into a climbing family. A carabiner had served as her diaper pin. For the others, the terrace seemed high and out of reach.

Of all people, Ben put an end to the argument. "I'll go first," he announced. He was no daredevil — in fact, he was a wimp and proud of it. But he sensed something familiar in Pitch's initiative. It was Griffin's can-do attitude, his fearless willingness to try anything to keep an operation moving along. Most of the time, that personality trait gave Ben nightmares. Yet, right then, he missed it so badly it was almost a physical ache.

Up the trellis he went, ignoring the scratch of rose thorns and the restless animal scrambling around inside his shirt. Near the top, a wave of drowsiness almost put him under — his narcolepsy was always worse in moments of stress. Just as he was nodding off, Pitch reached down and gripped his wrist. At that moment, Ferret Face came through with his trademark wake-up nip. The jolt of adrenaline provided the energy boost Ben needed to heave himself up the wall and — with Pitch's help — spill onto the balcony floor.

The others followed one by one. Savannah's ascent was a little shaky, since she carried Penelope under one arm. But with Pitch pulling from above and Victor pushing from below, she made it to the terrace. Melissa brought up the rear, climbing with confidence and determination. For the shy girl, this was the easy part. Party crashing was a lot scarier than falling — even off a thousand-foot cliff.

Victor opened the French doors, and the music from inside quadrupled in volume. "The plan is simple — find

Grant Bruckman. It's pretty loud in there, so we're going to have to shout to get noticed."

"And keep a low profile," Pitch added. "Remember that lunkhead at the front door. We don't belong, so if anybody gets suspicious, try to disappear into the crowd."

"Not a problem," Logan said confidently. "My character is complete. I'm a thirteen-year-old grad student with an IQ of two hundred and fifty. I'm majoring in infrared astronomy, and my goal is to make contact with an alien race."

"Try looking in the mirror," Ben told him sourly.

"It's four fifteen," Victor told them. "If the ticket's here, we'll have just enough time to get it to the lottery office by six."

The team entered the house and started down the long hallway. Ahead they could see the party crowd looping up the stairs onto the second-floor landing. Ben peered over the rail. The living room was a boiling mass of dancers, the music so loud that he felt every drumbeat and thrum of bass in his sinuses. An agitated Ferret Face burrowed into his armpit in an attempt to escape the noise.

"There are, like, a million people here!" he exclaimed, raising his voice to be heard.

"We'll split up," Victor announced. "Six of us can cover more ground. If you find Bruckman, give a signal and we'll all come together. We'll probably have to search his room for the ticket."

"What signal?" Pitch demanded. "You couldn't hear a cannon shot in this place!"

Then Victor Phoenix proved beyond any doubt that he could be *a* Man With a Plan, even if he'd never be the main one. "When you've got him, pull the plug out of the stereo, and the rest of us will come after you. Okay, let's go."

The group dispersed into the tightly packed revelers, fighting the human current to make their way down to the main level.

"Do you know Grant Bruckman?" Ben asked the first face that turned his way.

"Everybody knows the Bruckmeister," the young man replied. "What are you, his kid brother?"

Ben ignored the question and pressed on. "Is he here at the party?"

"I saw him on the dance floor, but that was, like, an hour ago."

"Can you describe him?" Ben persisted.

The college student's eyes narrowed. "You ask a lot of nosy questions for a little shrimp."

Ben backed off and pushed farther down the steps. The last thing he needed was to make a scene and get thrown out.

Logan was near the bottom of the stairs. "I'm looking for Grant Bruckman," he explained to several Sigma Delta Phis. "He's in my infrared astronomy class."

"Yeah, right," snorted one of them. "What are you, twelve?"

"Thirteen, actually," the young actor replied, pleased to be able to transition into character so early in the conversation. "I go here because my enormous intellect has already absorbed everything they could teach me in middle or high school."

"Hey!" crowed another brother. "Get a load of the dweeb!"

"Dweeb?" Logan was offended. "I got a perfect score on my SATs!"

"Let's get him!"

On the spot, Logan decided to add a running-away dimension to his character's personality. If there was one thing he'd learned about the theatre, it was that an actor had to be able to think on his feet. He quickly disappeared into the throng.

Of the six of them, Pitch was covering the most ground. She squeezed through the dance floor, staring brazenly into faces and shouting, *Grant Bruckman?* She wasn't getting many answers, but the occasional pointing finger guided her in what she hoped was the right direction.

Savannah was attracting attention with Penelope in her arms. But unfortunately, that was coming from girls, none of whom could be Grant. Poor Melissa was making the least progress of any of them. Even bellowing directly into someone's ear, she simply could not muster enough volume to make herself heard over the blasting music.

It took forever for Ben to work his way downstairs.

He had to walk backward to avoid bumping Ferret Face against the endless stream of revelers. The concealed creature had been whacked, jostled, and crushed into Ben's stomach so many times that he was hissing and spitting nonstop.

Something grabbed Ben's ankle, and he jumped, nearly causing his ferret to abandon shirt. Bewildered, he looked under a table piled high with pizza boxes. There crouched Logan, a furtive expression in his eyes.

"Logan — what are you doing down there?"

"Hiding!" Logan hissed. "Those guys are after me!"

"For asking about Grant Bruckman?"

"They're jealous of me because I'm a genius!" Logan said resentfully. "Today's college kids have got no respect!"

"But you're *not* a genius," Ben reminded him. "You're just pretending."

"An actor has to get into character," Logan asserted in defense of his art. "It's not the kind of thing you can turn on and off like a light switch."

Ben reached down and hauled the boy to his feet, whacking his head on the tabletop in the process. "Never mind acting! We need everybody on the search!"

Logan drew himself up stiffly. "A performer can't work under such stressful conditions."

"*There he is!*" bellowed a voice from the dining room.

Three big Sigma Delta Phis were plowing through the crowd, intent on recapturing Logan.

The speed with which the young actor got out of the line of fire was worthy of Houdini. It left Ben standing beside the table, defenseless. Two of the three frat brothers broke through and grabbed him. One under each arm, they lifted him high off the floor.

"Wrong kid!" the third brother objected.

"What difference does it make?" the captor on the left shot back. "Right kid, wrong kid — he's going for a swim."

"Put me down!" Ben wailed. "You're scaring my ferret!"

The third brother swept him by the ankles, and the trio began to carry him across the turbulent dance floor.

"Hey, that's not right!" Victor began to push his way toward the airborne Ben.

"Beat it or you're next!" A vicious shove slammed Victor into two dancers, who bounced him in another direction like a human pinball. He jumped up and tried to muscle his way back to Ben, but it was impossible to buck the crowd.

Tears of anger and frustration sprang to Victor's eyes. He had been the victim of this kind of treatment in the past. And now he was helpless to keep it from happening to his friend.

"This is college, kid," the Sigma Delta Phi told Griffin. "Nobody wastes their time buying lottery tickets. And, not for nothing, a piece of friendly advice — your backpack goes on your back. That's why they call it a *back*pack."

"There was a winning ticket sold to someone in this frat house!" Griffin insisted, tightening his grip on Luthor's leash. "Time is running out on a lot of money!"

"Give it to me," the young man replied readily. "I'm up to my nostrils in student loans."

"It doesn't work that way," said Griffin urgently. "You have to have the tick —"

A horrifying sight met his eyes. Three burly frat brothers dangled a slight figure over a huge tub filled with ice and meltwater. Griffin's breath caught in his throat.

The victim was Ben!

Without a thought, Griffin sprang to the aid of his best friend, but he made no progress in the crush of so many larger bodies. Desperately, he pushed Luthor ahead of him, opening up a pathway to the giant tin tub. He left his feet just as the frat boys raised Ben high over the meltwater and let go. With a squeal of terror, Ben hurtled toward the icy bath. Inches before splashdown, Griffin struck him in midair, knocking him clear of the slushy water and sending him rolling into a forest of legs on the dance floor.

The bolt of frigid lightning that shot through Griffin as he went into the ice up to his knees was nothing compared with the fear he felt for the safety of his father's invention. If those delicate electronics got wet, the SweetPick would fry — and so would Griffin when Dad got through with him. In an impressive demonstration of full-body muscle control, he sprang free of the drink and toppled out of the tub beside Ben. He probably wouldn't have made it if Victor had not been there to give him a boost over the side.

Luthor turned sheepdog, circling Griffin, Ben, and Victor, daring one and all to approach them. Nobody did.

Victor regarded Griffin in awe. "You saved him!"

"W-what are you g-guys d-doing here?" stammered Griffin, teeth chattering from the cold.

At that moment, the blaring music went silent. After the pounding roar of hip-hop, the sudden silence seemed even louder and more jarring.

"The signal!" Victor exclaimed. His eyes traveled to the stereo on the far wall. But it was no member of his team standing there holding the plug.

"*Mike?*" Griffin exclaimed in disbelief.

The hippie storekeeper's face radiated deep purpose as he towered over everyone in his tie-dye glory. He threw down the cord and hefted an electric guitar.

"Dudes, dudes!" Mike's eyes were wide above his bushy beard. "This whole scene is a total downer! It's all about me, me, me — *my* party, *my* girlfriend, *my* slice of pizza, *my* good time! That's not what we fought for in the sixties. That's not why we held sit-ins and be-ins, and faced down the National Guard with nothing but flower power!"

A confused murmur buzzed through the crowd.

"Whose grandfather is that?"

"Isn't he the guy from the convenience store?"

"What's he doing with my guitar?"

"And these *songs*," Mike pleaded. "They're not about protest, or revolution, or touching people's souls. Whatever happened to the rock-and-roll titans who took the stage during those three days of peace and music in 1969?"

With that, he brought his right hand down on the strings of the guitar. A blast of noise and feedback erupted from the speakers that sent hands to cover ears all around the frat house. It was every bit as loud as what had come before, but more raw, discordant, and powerful. It was an onslaught of sound his audience could feel under their cuticles.

Mike launched into an earsplitting performance of Jimi Hendrix's electric version of "The Star-Spangled Banner." His fingers were just a blur as they raked the strings. Wailing guitar gave way to shrieking feedback.

Ferret Face sank his teeth into Ben's skin, not to wake him up but because of the assault on his sensitive hearing. Luthor chased his short tail. Partygoers winced in pain as the din swelled to an agonizing crescendo.

The first speaker sizzled and blew fifteen seconds into the performance. After that, they all followed, burning out one at a time, silencing the guitar. Smoke rose from the frying amps, forming a single cloud at the ceiling. The smoke detectors began to howl. They were substantially quieter than the guitar solo that had just been cut off.

Mike was still playing, oblivious to the fact that there was no sound. Darren grabbed the storekeeper's arm. "Let's get out of here! You want to be far from this place when they figure out who wrecked the party!"

Mike dropped the guitar and they joined the stampede for the exit.

Outside was chaos as the revelers ran for their lives. In the general confusion of (a) was the frat house burning down? (b) who was that old guy with the guitar? and (c) did the national anthem mean the party was over? the Cedarville contingent — including Darren and Mike — formed its own group in the crowd. At first, Luthor was delighted to see his beloved Savannah on the scene. But then he noticed that she carried Penelope in her arms, and he snubbed her and went to stand by the shivering Griffin. Savannah looked sad.

Ben turned to Griffin. "Your dad's invention — did it get wet?"

"It's fine." He shuddered. "I hope."

"Thanks, man. I don't think Ferret Face could have survived it."

"I hope *I* survive it!" Griffin snapped back. "What are you guys doing here, anyway?"

"It's a plan," Ben admitted, shamefaced. "We're looking for the missing Giga-Millions ticket."

Griffin was irritated. "That's *my* plan!"

"No, it's not," put in Pitch. "It's *Victor*'s plan."

"Actually," Victor admitted, "I got the idea from Darren. It's *his* plan."

Savannah bristled. "You mean all this time we've been working for *Darren Vader*?"

"Well, if you knew it was me, you never would have done it!" Darren said righteously.

"This is low, even for you," Griffin accused Darren. "You sent me off on a wild-goose chase, then hung me out to dry and recruited the others as backup."

Victor looked stricken. "You lied to me, Darren. You pretended you were the good guy, and anything bad was Griffin's fault. You let me believe he was a bully."

Darren shrugged. "I was going to cut everybody in for a share of the money."

"Don't forget the Woodstock monument," added Mike. "Today proves how much we need to remember the great moments of the past."

Darren nodded fervently. "It's not too late for all of us to get what we want! There's still time to find Grant Bruckman!"

"Find me for what?" asked a deep voice behind them.

Everybody turned. A slim college student in a Delta Sigma Phi hoodie regarded them quizzically. "Do I know you guys? How come you know me?" He panned the group, stopping at the storekeeper. "Oh, hi, Mike. Who are all these kids?"

"They're looking for you, man," Mike replied. "They think you're the missing Giga-Millions winner from last year."

Grant snorted. "Yeah, right. All the tickets I've bought from you, I've never won a cent. Not even once."

Griffin jumped in. "Are you sure?" he pressed. "It's easy to forget to check the numbers one week out of a whole year."

Grant laughed bitterly. "Ever been a poor student, kid? In debt up to your eyeballs, living on ramen noodles? Yeah, I check the numbers — with an electron microscope. Sorry, but you've got the wrong millionaire."

And Grant Bruckman — their last hope — returned to his friends.

Griffin panned the group with a resentful expression. "Now you see what happens when you try to pull off something big without a real planner!"

That was too much for Ben. "You can't blame this on Victor. His plan failed because he was searching for something that just wasn't there, same as you. You may be The Man With The Plan, but other people are allowed to have ideas, too."

"At least Victor's a team player," Pitch added reproachfully. "He takes suggestions from people, talks things over. No offense, Griffin, but you're like King Bing, high exalted dictator and control freak. What you say goes, and nobody else matters."

"Cooperation, man," Mike put in. "After peace and love, that's what made the sixties work."

Griffin was about to fire back in anger when he experienced a moment of chagrin that very nearly flattened him.

They were right. It was all true. He was so dead set on running the show that he'd turned into a tyrant. He'd bulldozed the team into Operation Treasure Hunt to get back at Darren, and look where that had landed all of them. If he'd taken a minute to listen to their objections . . .

"Fair enough," he said finally. "Let's cooperate."

On the spot, The Man With The Plan did something he'd never done before: He revealed every detail of Operation Jackpot, going back to the very beginning, including every suspect he'd interviewed.

Victor spoke up next, outlining the ticket search from the others' point of view. It was obvious that the two factions had crossed paths several times on the hunt, and had probably come perilously close to treading on one another's toes. They had visited many of the same homes, and in some cases had been yelled at by suspects who didn't appreciate answering the same questions twice.

"Like that motorcycle guy," said Logan. "Some people just don't understand good acting."

"I was kicked out of a few places, too," Griffin admitted. "When they told me a kid had already been there, I figured it was Vader."

"The meanest by far was that Tobias Fielder," Victor complained. "You remember, with the house full of junk and all those hanging plants."

Pitch laughed. "He's just crabby because he's afraid the library is going to come and seize his gazillion overdue books."

"He creeped me out," Savannah chimed in, cradling Penelope. "He had so many library notices, he was using them as bookmarks."

"Not just library notices," Ben added. "Also business cards, Post-it notes, cash register receipts —"

Suddenly, Griffin saw the answer burst out of itself like a kernel of microwave popcorn.

"And *lottery tickets*!" cried The Man With The Plan.

G riffin wheeled on the others, eyes wide with dis-
covery and excitement. "Don't you see? The guy's
got stuff all over the place — he doesn't know what's
in there! The FBI couldn't keep track of the junk in
that house. When he needs a bookmark, he grabs the
nearest piece of paper, regardless of whether it's a
card, or an envelope —"

"Or a Giga-Millions ticket!" Victor finished
breathlessly.

"We've got to get back there!" Griffin exclaimed.
"Mike — we need a ride to —"

Melissa already had the address up on her smartphone. "Sixty-eight Van Buren."

Abandoning the bikes on the frat house lawn, the
entire group piled into the Volkswagen bus. It was a
tight squeeze to get eight middle schoolers, a very tall
hippie, a giant Doberman, a cat, and a ferret into the
vehicle, but soon Mike was burning rubber away from
Swandon. Griffin kept a hand over the SweetPick's

power switch. Even without the Safe-chete blade, an accidental deployment could do a lot of damage with so many people and animals in such close quarters. Savannah reached out a tentative hand and stroked her beloved Doberman's short fur. He allowed this, if only because there was no other place to put his great head.

As they crossed into Green Hollow, Ben peered out the van's flyspecked window. "Hey, Griffin, isn't that your dad's car? What's he doing here?"

Griffin's head shrunk into his collar. "Looking for me. I ran out on a field test for the SweetPick."

Melissa offered her phone. "Call him."

"I can't — not in the middle of a plan. He'd come after me and slow us down. We've only got forty minutes left."

"If we find the ticket but run out of time and lose the money, I'll never forgive myself," Darren vowed.

"You'll have company," Pitch assured him. "We'll never forgive you, either."

Everyone held on as the bus wheeled around the corner onto Van Buren Street and screeched to a halt in front of the debris-strewn lawn. Like the occupants of a clown car at the circus, team members poured out of the VW from every opening and raced to the front door.

Griffin rang the bell several times. "Mr. Fielder!" he called, hearing movement inside the house. "Let us in!"

"It's an emergency!" cried Victor. "You won the lottery!"

"Again!" added Darren. "You're so lucky —" His voice broke. "You got all the luck! You didn't leave any for the rest of us —"

Pitch clapped her hand over his mouth just as the door swung wide and Tobias Fielder's macramé cap appeared out of the jungle of hanging plants. "What are you talking about? I won years ago."

"You won *again*!" Griffin babbled, feeling the time pressure. "But the ticket expires at six! Let us in so we can find it for you!"

"Well, okay. But not the dog. Or the cat." He took in Ferret Face poking out of Ben's shirt. "Or whatever that is."

"He's a medical necessity," Ben insisted, pushing inside with the others.

Luthor and Penelope were left alone on the porch. They kept their distance, regarding each other with suspicion.

Inside the cluttered house, the search of the books began in earnest. There were hundreds of them, piled on tables, chairs, countertops, and the floor. A few even swung in macramé planters. It seemed an insurmountable task, but Griffin and Victor had briefed the team on efficient hunting techniques and division of responsibility. Only books were examined, and only for bookmarks. They found mail and receipts dating back to the 1980s, papers yellowed with age, unpaid bills, candy wrappers, all jammed in, marking the reader's page. There were Post-its, Kleenex, and squares of toilet paper. Business cards, playing cards, baseball cards, even a tarot card. But no lottery ticket.

"Are you sure that's everything?" Griffin cried, watching the time. The house was a maze of flotsam and jetsam, but it was not overly large. In fourteen minutes, the team had gone through every book and magazine.

Mike was curious. "How come you have so many overdue books?"

Mr. Fielder looked surprised. "I don't have overdue books."

"Oh, come on!" Darren exploded, the pressure getting to him with every tick of the clock. "What do you call these?"

The homeowner stuck out his jaw, insulted. "I'm very organized. I just took a batch back to the library yesterday."

The team surveyed the disorder of the house. Was Mr. Fielder really so weird that he honestly didn't see the chaos all around him? That he didn't notice the forest for the trees — the books for the other stuff? In that case, it would be easy to see how he might overlook a thirty-million-dollar ticket.

"Wait a minute." Victor spoke up. "You returned some books *yesterday*?"

Griffin was already high-stepping through the bric-a-brac for the door. "Mike, where's the library around here?"

"Way ahead of you, man." The tall hippie winced as his head whacked a low-hanging planter.

They collected the dog and cat on the porch and piled back into the VW, which started in a cloud of burning oil. Mr. Fielder followed in the van with the macramé in the windows.

The time was 5:38. Only twenty-two minutes remained before the deadline.

30

Ten humans and three animals barreled full bore into the Green Hollow Public Library. It was a major invasion, yet the librarian at the desk had eyes only for the man in the handmade cap.

"You!" she seethed, drawing herself up to her full height of five feet. "You are not welcome in this building!"

Tobias Fielder spread his arms in a gesture of innocence. "What did I do?"

"There are many reasons patrons don't return materials on time," she stormed, wagging a bony finger. "They misplace them, or forget due dates — all honest mistakes. You have elevated overdue books to crime-of-the-century level!"

"I was just at the book drop yester —"

"It will cost this branch a fortune to replace what you've walked away with," she accused. "Your overdue fines alone are more than two thousand dollars!"

Griffin spoke up. "He can afford it! At least, he'll be able to! Just take us to yesterday's book-drop books!"

"I'm sorry," she told him. "Materials returned yesterday have already been reshelved."

"It's no use, Griffin," said Ben. "We'll never have time to search the whole library. We've only got eighteen minutes."

Darren was in agony. "You don't give up on thirty million dollars!"

"You're better off without it," Mike told him. "Look how uptight you are. Your chakras are completely out of alignment."

"Yeah?" Darren retorted. "Don't forget your Woodstock monument circling the bowl!"

The tall hippie shrugged. "As Bob Dylan said, 'When you've got nothing, you've got nothing to lose.'"

But Griffin was unwilling to admit defeat. He had been through too much on account of this phantom lottery ticket. He had been labeled a bully and forced to pick up garbage in every back alley in Cedarville. He had run off on Dad with an unpatented prototype still strapped to his midsection, leaving a vital component abandoned in a field. He had even teamed up with the likes of Darren Vader. Worst of all, this caper had nearly cost him his friends, and nothing was worth that.

The whole world had been turned upside down, and there was only one way to make things right again. He

had to do what The Man With The Plan always did —
see an operation through to the end.

He turned to Mr. Fielder. "What books did you return
yesterday? If they've been reshelved, we can find them."

"I'm completely organized," said Mr. Fielder for the
umpteenth time. He frowned as his completely organized mind shut down completely.

Griffin stared at him and faced an unhappy fact.
There was nothing under that macramé cap but air.

And then he realized he was staring right at it. He
wheeled on the librarian. "The books returned yesterday — were any of them about macramé?"

She consulted the computer at the reception desk.
"One," she reported. "*Why Knot: The Art of Macramé.*
Dewey decimal number 746.4." By the time she looked
up, she was talking to herself.

Griffin led the stampede to the seven hundreds.
When they found the right shelf, they jammed into the
aisle, scanning spines and reading numbers.

"*It isn't there!*" wailed Darren.

A chorus of "Shhhh!" came from all around them.

"But it's supposed to be here!" Griffin heaved in
consternation.

"Maybe it got shelved in the wrong place," Melissa
suggested.

This prompted a wild inspection of the nearby
stacks, which had books flying in all directions and
strewn about the carpet.

Another librarian appeared, this one furious. "What's going on here?"

"I'll tell you what's going on," Darren rasped. "You owe me thirty million dollars!"

The angry woman ignored him. "What is that dog doing here? And the cat? No pets in the library!"

"We'll take them right out," Griffin promised. "But we need a book first. It's called *Why Knot: The Art of Macramé*. It's supposed to be here, but it isn't."

"Well, either someone checked it out —" Multiple gasps of horror seemed to come from a single agonized throat. "Or," she continued, "it might be on the bookmobile."

"Bookmobile?" Victor wheezed.

"Our driver just loaded up a fresh shipment. If you hurry, you might be able to catch her in the parking lot."

If there had been an Olympic speed record for exiting a library, the team would have shattered it. Pitch hit the sidewalk first, Griffin hot on her heels, Luthor loping behind him. They started for the parking lot just as a white panel truck motored up the driveway and merged into traffic. On the side was the logo of the Green Hollow Public Library along with the message: BOOKS ON BOARD.

"*No-o-o-o-o!!!*" Darren's cry was barely human.

Griffin, Ben, Victor, Pitch, Savannah, Logan, Melissa, Darren, Mike, and Mr. Fielder sprinted after the bookmobile, screaming at top volume. Ferret Face burrowed deep inside Ben's sleeve and dug in his little claws, hanging on for dear life. Luthor's long strides soon brought him to the front of the pack. Not to be outdone, Penelope leaped out of Savannah's arms and hit the pavement running, matching the big dog's pace.

The truck was accelerating, opening up an insurmountable lead. Griffin's eyes took in the clock on the bank tower ahead. Twelve minutes to go. If the bookmobile got away from them here, it would all be over.

There was only one hope: the traffic light at the next intersection. It had to turn red. It just had to.

The truck roared on. The light remained green.

Come on — change!

At the last second, the signal turned yellow. The rev of the engine swelled as the driver prepared to run the light. Then, at the last second, she thought better of it, and the bookmobile squealed to a stop.

The pursuers stampeded down the block in a desperate bid to reach the panel truck before the light changed again. They almost made it. Dog and cat were at the corner when the green signal returned. Traffic resumed. There was a grinding noise as the bookmobile shifted back into drive.

Luthor was streetwise, and pulled up, but Penelope ran right out in front of the library vehicle.

"Penelope!" chorused Savannah and Victor in terror as the van burst forward.

Luthor did not hesitate. In a single titanic bound, he leaped into the path of the truck and picked up the cat by her collar. In a spectacular display of canine agility, he hurled himself and his bitter enemy back onto the sidewalk just as the bookmobile roared into the space they'd occupied a split second before. Had he acted an instant later, both animals would have been struck.

With a cry, the mobile librarian slammed on the brakes. The truck lurched to a halt.

Darren was not going to wait for an engraved invitation. He threw open the sliding side door and jumped aboard.

The driver, already badly shaken by her near miss with the animals, could only gasp. "What do you want?"

"*Why Knot: The Art of Macramé!*" He attacked the built-in shelves, hunting frantically, chucking books in all directions.

The others swarmed the vehicle, joining the search.

Savannah's arms were locked around Luthor's strong neck. "Oh, sweetie, I've never been so proud of you! Risking your life to save Penelope after everything that's happened — you're a hero!"

The cat walked back and forth, rubbing up against the Doberman's flank in a gesture of gratitude and affection. Luthor looked supremely pleased with himself.

The mobile librarian was in a terrible state. "You can't be here! Those books are town property! This is against the rules!" Her gaze fell on Mr. Fielder. "I should have known! You haven't got enough of our materials already — you have to hijack the bookmobile!"

Mr. Fielder was mystified. "What's everybody so mad at me for? I'm a very big reader!"

Kindly, Mike helped the overwrought librarian slide over to the passenger seat and replaced her behind the wheel. "I'll drive. You just relax. Do you know any meditation techniques?"

"Take us to the lottery office!" Griffin called from the midst of the search. "We haven't found the ticket yet, but when we do, we need to be right there."

"There's only six minutes to go!" moaned Darren.

Mike put the truck in gear. "Don't worry, it's not far."

Pitch slammed the sliding door shut and the bookmobile squealed around in a wide, illegal U-turn. The searchers were tossed every which way, but nothing could interrupt their concentration. There were more than four hundred books on the shelves — a big number, but not an impossible one. If they kept their cool, they'd find it.

As a lottery vendor, Mike had been to the office countless times and knew all the shortcuts. Still, every stop sign and red light cost them precious seconds. The minutes ticked down from four, to three, to two.

"Are we close?" wheezed Darren, near hysterics.

"It doesn't matter if we haven't got the ticket," Pitch snapped irritably.

And then a small voice said, "Macramé."

It was Victor. "*Why Knot: The Art of Macramé*! This is it — and there's a bookmark in it!"

Carefully, as if he were handling a delicate butterfly specimen, he removed the slip of paper. As crowded as they were in the back of the bookmobile, the group squeezed even closer, staring, hoping.

It was a Giga-Millions ticket from the drawing held October 6. Barely daring to breathe, Griffin examined the numbers.

12 . . . 17 . . . 18 . . . 34 . . . 37 . . . 55 . . .

"We've got it," he said, more calmly than he would have believed possible.

"One minute!" squeaked Ben.

They had the ticket, but would they have the time?

"We're here!" called Mike, slowing before a small row of storefronts. "It's right across the street!"

Darren was overcome with emotion. "It's the most

beautiful thing I've ever seen," he told Victor. "Can I hold it?"

"*Don't!*" chorused Griffin, Ben, Pitch, Savannah, Logan, and Melissa.

Mike glanced over his shoulder. "What's wrong?"

Crash! The bookmobile rear-ended a station wagon that was cruising the block at slow speed. An angry man jumped out.

"Griffin," Ben exclaimed. "It's your dad!"

And then Darren Vader snatched the winning ticket from Victor's hand, heaved the sliding door open, jumped out, and began to run for the lottery office across the street.

"No!"

Griffin blasted after him, the team following in furious agony. After everything that had happened, no way could they let this money-grubbing backstabber cash in the ticket himself.

Mr. Bing looked up from the dented rear bumper of his car just in time to see his missing son flash by, wearing his missing prototype. "Griffin?"

But Griffin could not slow down — could not even waste a syllable to acknowledge his father. Darren was already halfway across the street, the open doorway of the lottery office thirty feet away.

Once again, big Darren's football training made him difficult to catch up to. Griffin's ragged breath came out in wild gasps. His lungs were on fire. Worse, he was slowed down by the SweetPick, which was a burden, even without the steel Safe-chete blade.

It struck him like a cannon shot: *There's no Safe-chete blade!*

Propelled by a depth of determination he scarcely could have imagined, Griffin put on a burst of acceleration that drew him right on Darren's heels. The lottery office beckoned just a few strides ahead. It was now or never.

With a silent prayer, Griffin reached down and flicked the dangling switch on his father's invention.

32

With its telltale *flack*, the SweetPick did exactly what it was designed to do. There wasn't a blade to slice the sugarcane at its base, but the U-Bundle mechanism flung out a length of twine and, lassoing Darren from behind, cinched tight, tying his arms to his sides.

"Awesome!" whispered Mr. Bing, watching his invention in action.

The shock of this assault threw off Darren's balance. The big boy went down with a half-demented shriek. So great was his momentum that he tumbled and rolled clear past the lottery office door. He lost his grip on the ticket, and thirty million dollars was fluttering in the breeze over a sewer drain.

With a cry of purpose, Pitch left her feet in an athletic dive, her arms straining to catch the ticket in midair. She hit the ground just as the slip dropped through the grating. At the last minute, she jammed her fingers into the opening and somehow managed to trap the precious paper against the underside of the iron grill.

Griffin was devastated. "We *lost* it?"

Very slowly and carefully, Pitch drew her hand out of the sewer, the multimillion-dollar ticket pinched between her middle and index fingers.

Inside the storefront of the lottery office, the lights went out abruptly.

Ben stared at his watch in horror. "Ten seconds!"

Flaked out on the sidewalk, Pitch could only hold out the ticket. Victor snatched it from her and passed it to Griffin, who ran for the entrance.

Through the glass of the lottery office, they could see the clerk closing the front door.

"Wait!" howled Griffin in anguish. He wasn't going to make it —

In desperation, Melissa whipped her smartphone out of her pocket and slid it along the sidewalk. The device skittered across the concrete and slipped inside the steel frame just as the heavy door came around.

The case dented; the screen cracked. But the door remained open a few inches.

It was all the time Griffin needed. He burst into the lottery office at 5:59:58, October 6, two seconds to expiration.

Wordlessly, Griffin slapped the ticket into the clerk's hand.

At first, she seemed irritated to be bothered so close to closing time. "Couldn't this wait till tomorrow?"

"No!" Griffin croaked. The long elaborate story formed in his brain, but he was so physically and mentally exhausted that he could only point to the slip and rasp, "Check it out."

She noticed the date first, and then the numbers. "This is it! This is the one! Why would you delay so long? Another few seconds and I would have locked you out!"

Griffin could only shake his head. He didn't have the strength for this explanation, either. As she registered the ticket in the Giga-Millions machine, the small office began to fill up. First came Victor, the team, and Darren, trussed up like a Thanksgiving turkey. They were followed by Mr. Fielder, Mike, and the bookmobile librarian. Bringing up the rear was Mr. Bing. As he held the door open, Luthor and Penelope slipped inside. They curled up in a corner in perfect harmony and watched the humans go through their paces.

Mr. Bing sidled up to his son. "Griffin, what's going on?"

Griffin pointed to Mr. Fielder. "That guy is the missing thirty-million-dollar winner. We found the ticket for him." He shrugged out of the SweetPick. "Oh, yeah, and I field-tested your invention. Darren helped."

"I saw that," his father chortled. "Those Brazilians are going to be eating out of my hand."

Nobody made a move to unwrap Darren.

The clerk spoke up. "Who is the owner of the ticket?"

Mr. Fielder stepped forward. "That would be me."

Darren began to jump up and down. "It's mine! I'm trying to raise my hand, but they tied me up when they stole the ticket from me!"

The clerk frowned at him. "No one under eighteen can play the lottery."

"I'm small for my age!"

"He's annoying for his age," Pitch explained.

"He's annoying for any age," the clerk agreed. She addressed Mr. Fielder. "Sir, my advice to you is to call a lawyer, because you just became a very wealthy man. Congratulations."

Wild cheering erupted in the office. Griffin knew a thrill that had nothing to do with money. Operation Jackpot — the most incredible long shot of anything he'd ever attempted — had succeeded. It was almost as unlikely as winning the lottery itself, and every bit as satisfying.

"I don't need a lawyer," Mr. Fielder replied. "I'm extremely well organized."

It got a laughing cheer from the Cedarville crew and an exasperated rolling of eyes from the book-mobile librarian.

"Yeah, get a lawyer!" pleaded Darren. "My mom's a lawyer! Hire her!"

"Your mother's a patent lawyer, Darren," Mr. Bing reminded him.

"That's how good she is," Darren insisted. "She even gets patents for the dumb stuff *you* invent!"

"Give it up, Vader," groaned Ben, stroking Ferret Face beneath his T-shirt. "You're just trying to cut yourself in for a piece of the action."

"What's wrong with that?" Darren challenged. "We all deserve a cut of the money. If it weren't for us, that ticket would be stuck in a macramé book worth zero!"

"And don't forget the fund to create a national monument at Woodstock," Mike chimed in. "Nothing could be a worthier cause than that."

"Hold on! Hold on!" Mr. Fielder held up both hands. "It seems to me you folks have a lot of opinions on how to spend *my* jackpot. This isn't my first lottery win, you know. I'm wise to all the vultures who start circling as soon as there's a little cash to be had. Well, I've already made up my mind where the bulk of this money is going."

An expectant silence fell in the lottery office. Even Luthor and Penelope sat up at attention, sensing that something important was coming. Ferret Face peered out of Ben's collar. What was Mr. Fielder planning to do with thirty million dollars?

"Ever since my retirement, these wonderful people have kept my mind engaged and have provided a second home," announced the man in the macramé cap. "They're like family to me. That's why I'm planning to make a large donation to the Green Hollow Public Library."

The stunned silence in the lottery office was broken by a gasp from the bookmobile lady as she collapsed into the arms of Mr. Bing and fainted dead away.

O n October 7, the Green Hollow Public Library offi-cially forgave Mr. Tobias Fielder $2,274.75 in overdue fines. It was the least they could do. Thanks to his huge donation, the library was planning a major expansion. The staff also removed the DO NOT LEND TO THIS MAN signs, featuring his picture, from the check-out desks and — reluctantly — his personal dartboard from the break room.

"For that kind of money, he can steal any book he pleases, with our blessing," the chief librarian announced off the record.

Mr. Fielder was famous. The newspapers called him The Luckiest Man in America, and he was interviewed on all the TV networks about his second lottery win. Appearing on CNN in his trademark macramé cap, the big winner shrugged off questions about why he waited until the last second to claim his prize.

"I'm extremely organized," he assured the inter-viewer. "I knew exactly what I was doing."

He made no mention of the eight kids who had moved heaven and earth to track down his missing ticket against all odds. But that didn't mean the group from Cedarville was unappreciated. The team, Victor, and even Darren received generous donations to their college funds out of the Giga-Millions jackpot.

Darren's disappointment was bitter. "College fund!" he spat. "That ungrateful weirdo wouldn't have thirty cents if it weren't for me! And what do I get? Money I can't touch unless I spend it on extra school! It's enough to make a guy hurl!"

"You're lucky you got anything more than a kick in the pants after what you did," Pitch informed him.

Another large beneficiary of the lottery win was Mike's favorite cause — a national monument at Woodstock. "If society has to be obsessed with the almighty dollar," the hippie storekeeper commented, "then you might as well spend it commemorating something cool." The donation from Mr. Fielder put the monument fund over the top. There were no immediate plans to begin construction, though, since the volunteers were too laid back to think so far ahead.

There were also a few minor charges that Mr. Fielder was only too happy to make good on. A new smartphone was purchased for Melissa. Of all the miracles she had performed with technology, the greatest had turned out to be using her old phone to keep the lottery office door from closing.

Also two auto repairs: one station wagon — rear bumper; one bookmobile — front bumper.

Mr. Fielder kept a chunk of his winnings for "the necessities of life," which might have meant buying a bigger house so he could fill it with more stuff. He was also planning a major financial investment. He had made a deal with Mr. Bing to become a silent partner in the SweetPick business. He had no interest in sugarcane but believed that the device could be used in the harvesting of hemp, which would provide him with an endless supply of yarn for macramé.

None of this would have been possible if the SweetPick hadn't finally received its patent approval. Amateur video of the U-Bundle mechanism taking down Darren had put the trademark panel in such a good mood that the invention passed with flying colors. No one could be certain how the YouTube link had reached the patent office, but Melissa had been able to trace the e-mail to the computer in Mrs. Vader's law office.

"Well, what do you know?" Griffin commented. "Darren's mom really *is* a good lawyer."

Ferret Face was munching on his breakfast pepperoni when Ben turned up at Griffin's house the next morning.

"How's the big guy?" Ben asked.

"Pretty good," Griffin replied. "You know what? I think he understands what's happening today, and he's psyched." He handed Ben an enormous bag of dry dog food. "Can you carry that?"

"Can anybody?" Ben disappeared behind the towering package. "Don't even think about it," he told Ferret Face, who came out to investigate the good smell. "This isn't for you. It isn't for *fifty* of you."

Griffin clipped Luthor onto his leash, and the three started off, Ben straining under the kibble, and Griffin struggling with a gigantic sack filled with favorite pillows, blankets, dog toys, and Milk-Bones.

By the time they reached Honeybee Street, it took the combined strength of the two of them to keep Luthor from dragging them down the sidewalk, bouncing them off mailboxes and fire hydrants.

"Wow," Ben commented in a strained voice. "I guess it's a pretty big deal making up with your best friend — even if you're a dog."

"Best friends don't have to make up. They may take breaks, but they've always got it going on." Griffin peered intently at the smaller boy. "Right?"

"Right." The massive bag of dog food concealed Ben's broad smile.

Every tree and fence post at the Drysdale house was decorated with balloons and yellow ribbons. A banner across the porch declared: WELCOME HOME, LUTHOR. The Doberman couldn't read, obviously. Yet there was no question in his mind that all this fuss had something to do with him.

Then the front door was thrown open and there she

was, his adored Savannah, her face alight with joy. The whole team was on hand, including Victor, to witness this homecoming. He saw Cleopatra, and his new friend, Penelope. Even Lorenzo, the albino chameleon, who didn't get out much, had left the terrarium to greet him.

Quivering with excitement, Luthor eased back on his haunches, ready to launch himself at his loved ones. All at once, he hesitated, as if sensing that there was something that needed to be done first. He turned back to Griffin, sat down, and offered one paw.

Griffin held out his hand and the two shook, almost like two businessmen finalizing a deal. Then the big dog gave in to his impulses and flung himself into Savannah's arms, bowling out the welcoming committee in the doorway.

"Oh-sweetie-I-missed-you-so-much-I'm-so-glad-you're-back-where-you-belong . . . !"

There was a party, of course, featuring cupcakes for the humans and Luthor's favorite snack — Swedish meatballs.

"I heard on the news," Logan announced, "that they're thinking of making a TV movie based on Mr. Fielder's two lottery wins. I'm definitely trying out for the part."

Pitch laughed. "Have you noticed that he's a little older than you? Like fifty years?"

Logan shrugged. "With some makeup and a mac-ramé hat, I could pass for him in front of his own mother."

Savannah gestured to where a stuffed and contented Luthor lay flat on his back, Penelope curled up by his ear. "Look at them," she cooed, dreamy with happiness. "Who could have imagined that those two would end up getting along so well?"

Griffin turned to Victor. "Speaking of getting along, I owe you a big apology. I've been down on you ever since you came to Cedarville, and I'm sorry. I never gave you a chance."

Victor shook his head. "I'm the one who should be apologizing to you. I was wrong about you being a bully. Darren was a jerk about that, but I should have had the brains to make up my own mind. The way you stood up for Ben at the frat house — you're the total opposite of a bully."

Savannah was still focused on Penelope, who crawled onto Luthor's belly and fell contentedly asleep again. "Tell your dad's allergist not to hurry," she said to Victor. "As far as I'm concerned, Penelope can stay here forever."

Victor flushed red as a tomato. "I have kind of a confession to make about that. My father doesn't have allergies."

Ben was mystified. "So why did your cat have to come live with Savannah?"

"Well" — Victor was shamefaced — "she isn't exactly my cat, either."

Melissa parted her curtain of hair. "Whose cat is she?"

"I got her at the pet shop about twenty minutes before I brought her over here." He saw them staring at him openmouthed, and decided to come clean all the way. "After getting picked on so much in Bass Junction, I was determined to make friends in my new town. I saw you guys, and you were awesome, but it's hard to break into a tight-knit group. I needed a way in. And when I heard about Savannah and animals, I came up with the idea of Penelope."

The team was horrified.

"You lied to us!" exclaimed Savannah.

"Dude, that's cold!" added Pitch.

Ben was so shocked that Ferret Face appeared at his collar to investigate the disturbance. "We trusted you!"

Melissa retreated behind her hair, which was where she usually hid from confrontation.

"Does this mean you don't care about our Oscar predictions?" Logan asked in desolation.

"Of course I do!" Victor pleaded. "I care about all of you guys! That's why it's important for you to know the truth. It started out as a way to break into the group, but everything else is totally real!"

His heart in his eyes, Victor looked from face to face, seeing disbelief, anger, resentment, suspicion, and, in Melissa's case, nothing at all.

Only Griffin, his former enemy, wore a wide smile. "Hey, don't be so hard on him," he told his friends.

Ben blew his stack. "Are you crazy? He played us

like a piano — to the point where we even turned against you! Don't you understand what he did?"

Griffin grinned. "I understand perfectly, and you should, too. It was a plan — and a pretty good one." He threw an arm around Victor's shoulders. "The kid's a planner, just like me."

The team officially had its newest member.